Praise for *Zoo, or Letters Not about Love*

"Shklovsky revitalizes the traditional epistolary novel."—*Choice*

"*Zoo* is more than a moving evocation of the pain of exile and unrequited love
... it is also rich with literary history."—*New Leader*

"*Zoo* is an excellent example of experimentation with the narrative in the
1920s.... The style is futurist, for it turns the mechanical world into an
emblem of longing and frustrated love."—*Library Journal*

Books by Viktor Shklovsky in English Translation

ZOO
or Letters Not about Love

Viktor Shklovsky

Translated with an introduction by Richard Sheldon

Dalkey Archive Press

Originally published in Russian by the Helikon Publishing House, Berlin, 1923

Translated from the Russian and edited by Richard Sheldon
English edition copyright © 1971 by Cornell University
Introduction copyright © 1971 by Richard Sheldon

First Dalkey Archive edition, 2001

Library of Congress Cataloging-in-Publication Data

Shklovskii, Viktor Borisovich, 1893-1984.
  [Zoo. English]
  Zoo, or Letters not about love / Viktor Shklovsky ; translated with an introduction by Richard Sheldon.
     p.   cm.
  ISBN 1-56478-311-1 (alk. paper)
     I. Title: Zoo. II. Title: Letters not about love. III. Sheldon, Richard (Richard Robert) IV. Title.

PG3476.S488 Z323 2001
891.73'42—dc21

                                                                    2001028780

Partially funded by a grant from the Illinois Arts Council, a state agency.

Dalkey Archive Press books are published by the Center for Book Culture, a nonprofit organization with offices in Chicago and Normal, Illinois.

www.dalkeyarchive.com

Printed on permanent/durable acid-free paper and bound in the United States of America.

Translator's Preface

Zoo, or Letters Not about Love is the first English translation of the Russian novel *Zoo, ili Pis'ma ne o liubvi,* by Viktor Shklovsky. The original work has gone through five Russian editions, and it has been translated during the last decade into French, German, and Italian. The present work is an unabridged translation of the first Russian edition, which was published by Helikon in Berlin in 1923 while Shklovsky was living as an exile there. This translation contains letters that were later omitted, possibly for political reasons. Included here as the Addenda are the prefaces to the later editions and the five letters added in the second edition, making a complete presentation of all published parts of *Zoo.*

The four subsequent editions of the Russian work have been published since Shklovsky returned to the Soviet Union: the second by the Athens Publishing House of Leningrad in 1924; the third by the Publishing House of Leningrad Writers in 1929; then, after a long hiatus, the fourth in 1964 as part of Shklovsky's book of memoirs *Zhili-byli* (Once upon a Time), by the Soviet Writers' Publishing House in Moscow. A revised edition of *Zhili-byli* was issued by the same firm in 1966.

The second edition of *Zoo* was substantially different from the first. Twelve letters were omitted (1, 2, 3, 8, 10, 16, preface to 19, 19, 20, 21, 23, and 28), and five new letters were added. In the third edition, all the original letters were restored, with the exception of Letters 7 and 20, while the new letters were retained. The fourth and fifth editions, which are essentially identical, kept the same basic format as the third, except that one of the new letters (31 in this translation) was omitted. Large parts of earlier letters also were omitted from the fourth and fifth editions—in most cases, it would seem, for political reasons. Of special interest, in this respect, are the deletions from the elegy to Khlebnikov (Letter 4), the letter about Pasternak (17), the petition to the Central Committee of the Communist Party (29), and the letter about automobiles (30). All significant changes in the various editions are described in the notes at the end of this volume. A small circle at the beginning and end of a passage indicates that this portion of the letter was omitted in a later edition. Information about the omitted portions is given at the appropriate place in the notes.

The French version of *Zoo* (1963) is based on the first edition and therefore does not include the five letters and other material added after Shklovsky returned to the Soviet Union. The German translation (1965) is based on the fourth edition and therefore does not include the three letters and other controversial passages that various circumstances forced Shklovsky to omit. The Italian translation (1966), despite its claim to be based on the first edition, is actually based on the second edition and therefore does not include twelve letters from the first edition.

I completed this translation while spending the academic year 1969–1970 as a fellow at the Center for Advanced Study in Urbana, Illinois, and wish to express my appreciation to the Center and to the University of Illinois. I want to thank Sarah Burke, Richard Gustafson, and Assya Humesky for helping me decipher some of the cryptic allusions. I am grateful to Vladimir Markov for his invaluable advice about the sections of the book pertaining to Khlebnikov.

I also want to thank Antonia Glasse for checking the translation against the original and the staff of Cornell University Press for their many helpful suggestions. My colleagues Peter Jarotski and Basil Milovsoroff helped constantly with difficult translation problems. I also want to remember Karen, who participated in all the work involved, and Katy and John, who love zoos. Finally, I want to thank Dimitri von Mohrenschildt for permission to reprint the excerpts that appeared in the July 1970 and October 1970 issues of *The Russian Review.*

RICHARD SHELDON

Hanover, New Hampshire

Contents

The Fire and the Ants

I threw on the fire a rotten log, not noticing that the inside of it was densely populated with ants.

The log began to split open; the ants tumbled out, running to and fro in desperation. They ran up and down the surface of the log, writhing as the flames consumed them. I took hold of the log and rolled it to the edge of the fire. Now many ants escaped—they ran onto the sand, onto the pine needles.

But strangely enough, they didn't run away from the fire.

Hardly had they overcome their terror when they turned back, ran around in circles and—some force drew them back, back to their deserted native land! Many ran back up on the burning log, scurried around on it, and perished there.

Aleksandr Solzhenitsyn
"Etudes and Tiny Tales," 1964
Translated by Richard Sheldon

Introduction

I

At the end of World War I, conquered Berlin became a refuge for hordes of homeless Russians. Seven unbroken years of world war, revolution, and civil war had driven more than three million Russians from their native land. They flocked to western Berlin in such numbers that the Germans facetiously referred to Kurfürstendamm as Nepsky Prospekt—an anagram of Nevsky Prospekt, the main street of Petrograd, and NEP, the initials of the New Economic Policy launched by Lenin in February 1921. A popular anecdote of the time told about the German who, hearing nothing but Russian spoken on the Kurfürstendamm, suffered an attack of homesickness, returned to his apartment, and forthwith hanged himself.[1]

The war between Germany and Russia had culminated in the onerous Treaty of Brest-Litovsk, which Germany had imposed in March 1918 on a Bolshevik regime fighting desperately for survival. Very soon thereafter—in May 1919 —the victorious Allies dictated the Treaty of Versailles to the

[1] This story is reported by Gleb Struve in his book *Russkaia literatura v izgnanii* [Russian Literature in Exile] (New York, 1956), p. 25; chap. i provides many valuable insights into this period of the Russian emigration.

Germans. Defeated Germany and Communist Russia, both viewed as outlaws by America and Europe, were forced to form what Churchill called a "comradeship in misfortune." Relations between the two countries, severed at the time of the Armistice in November 1918, were restored by a trade agreement in May 1921. In April 1922, when both Germany and Russia were snubbed by the Allies at the Genoa Convention, they withdrew from the meetings to sign the Treaty of Rapallo, which provided for complete resumption of diplomatic ties. Between 1923 and 1933, this partnership enabled Germany to circumvent the Treaty of Versailles by secretly producing arms and training officers in Russia.

The special relationship between the two countries made Berlin an advantageous location for the refugees, many of whom had not definitely decided to remain abroad. Even the tribulations of exile, though, failed to resolve the factionalism that had prevented effective concerted action against the Bolsheviks during the civil war. In June 1921, the so-called Reichenhall Congress was convened in an attempt to close ranks against the common enemy, but the right-wing émigré circles could not even agree on a single pretender to the throne. All except the most rabid elements did, however, resist the attempts of the nascent Nazi party to gain their support. Any tentative collaboration between the two groups terminated after Hitler's abortive putsch in November 1923.[2]

Conservative elements—monarchists of every hue (except

[2] See Walter Laqueur, *Russia and Germany: A Century of Conflict* (Boston and Toronto, 1965); Louis Fischer, *Russia's Road from Peace to War* (New York, Evanston, and London, 1969); E. H. Carr, *German-Soviet Relations between the Two World Wars*

red)—dominated Russian Berlin until 1922, when the arrival of many influential liberals altered the complexion of the colony. The influx was the result of three important events: 1) the transfer of the Smena Vekh (Changing Landmarks) faction from Paris to Berlin in March; 2) the showcase trial of Socialist Revolutionary leaders in Moscow during the summer; 3) the expulsion of more than 160 dissident intellectuals from Russia in the fall.

The Smena Vekh was a group of intellectuals heartened by the mellowing of communism which they discerned in the advent of NEP. These men got their name from the title of some essays published in the summer of 1921—essays in which they urged acceptance of the Bolshevik regime on the grounds that the Bolsheviks were, after all, the de facto rulers of Russia and heir to the country's national traditions. The Bolsheviks, hoping to retrieve some of the trained manpower lost in the exodus, subsidized the operations of Smena Vekh and permitted chapters to be organized inside Russia.

In the fall of 1921, the organization, centered in Paris, began publishing a weekly journal, also called *Smena Vekh*. In March 1922, this operation was transferred to Berlin, where the journal began to appear under the name *Nakanune* (On the Eve). The group made every effort to proselytize the Russian colony in Berlin. A prevalent theme of their campaign was the contrast between the decadence of Europe and the vitality of the new Russia—a theme also central to *Zoo*, though Shklovsky did not support or admire the Smena Vekh. Indeed, their efforts gained few converts in Berlin—with the notable

(New York, 1966); Hajo Holborn, *A History of Modern Germany, 1840–1945* (New York, 1969).

exception of Aleksei Tolstoy. By mid-1924, the movement was defunct, though it lingered inside Russia until the end of 1926.[3]

The second event that contributed liberal elements to Russian Berlin was the SR trial of June 1922.[4] The preparations for this trial and its results led to the flight and expulsion of a new wave of Russians—this time, mainly Mensheviks and Socialist Revolutionaries. It was this event which forced Shklovsky to flee. He had not endeared himself to the regime by his activities as futurist, formalist critic, and tutor of the Serapion Brothers. But, above all, he had sided with the SR party after the February revolution and served as a commissar in Kerensky's Provisional Government. In 1918, he had engaged in underground work against the Bolsheviks as part of a plot to restore the Constituent Assembly. He had been exonerated of charges resulting from these activities in 1919 through the intervention of Gorky, but he narrowly escaped arrest in March 1922 when the charges were reinstated and Gorky was no longer there to intercede for him. After lying low in Petrograd for a few weeks, he fled across the ice to Finland in May and then made his way to Berlin in early June. All these events are vividly described in his memoirs *Sentimental'noe puteshestvie* (A Sentimental Journey), which ends with his arrival in Berlin.[5]

[3] See Robert C. Williams, " 'Changing Landmarks' in Russian Berlin, 1922–1924," *Slavic Review*, XXVII (1968), 581–593.

[4] See David Shub, "The Trial of the SRs," *Russian Review*, XXIII (1964), 362–369.

[5] Viktor B. Shklovsky, *Sentimental'noe puteshestvie* (Moscow and Berlin, 1923; 2d ed. abr., Leningrad, 1924; 3d ed. abr., Moscow, 1929; English trans. by Richard Sheldon, Ithaca and London, 1970).

The Russian colony was at its zenith when Shklovsky arrived in the summer of 1922. Almost all the finest prose writers of the prerevolutionary period had emigrated, and most of them had settled in Berlin, which was recognized as the literary capital of the Russian diaspora. Even those writers and artists who remained in Russia visited Berlin frequently during the early twenties to participate in the stimulating cultural life of the Russian enclave. In *Zoo*, Shklovsky includes thumbnail sketches of Aleksei Remizov, Zinovy Grzhebin, Andrei Bely, Pyotr Bogatyryov, Ivan Puni (Jean Pougny), Marc Chagall, Ilya Ehrenburg, and Boris Pasternak, but this is only a partial list of the prominent Russians who frequented Berlin during those years. An indignant Maksim Gorky had left Russia in October 1921, when Lenin became increasingly impervious to his influence; Gorky settled in Saarow, a village on the outskirts of Berlin, and played a leading role in the activities of the Russian colony. The poet Sergei Esenin passed through Berlin in May 1922 with his most recent wife, the famous American dancer Isadora Duncan. Vladimir Mayakovsky spent the fall of 1922 in Berlin and participated actively in the intellectual life of the Russian colony; when he returned home, he reported on conditions of life there and specifically mentioned Shklovsky's deep despair at being separated from Russia.[6] Aleksei Tolstoy moved from Paris to Berlin in the fall of 1921 and remained there until his return to Russia in the spring of 1923. Vladimir Nabokov, whose family had escaped from Russia in May 1919, frequently visited his parents in Berlin while completing his studies at Cambridge. (His father, leader of the Kadet party,

[6] Vladimir Mayakovsky, *Polnoe sobranie sochinenii* [Complete Collected Works] (13 vols.; Moscow, 1955–1961), XII, 463.

was assassinated by Russian right-wing extremists in March 1922 while addressing a convention of émigrés called to find ways of alleviating the terrible famine in Russia.) Nabokov, already publishing poetry in Berlin periodicals under the name V. Sirin, settled permanently in Berlin during 1923 and used the Russian colony as the setting for his first novel, *Mashenka*, 1926. Marina Tsvetaeva spent the summer of 1922 in Berlin on her way to exile in Prague.

Ehrenburg recalls those turbulent days in his memoirs:

There existed one place in Berlin reminiscent of Noah's Ark, where the clean and the unclean met peaceably; it was called the House of Arts. Russian writers congregated in this ordinary German café on Fridays. Tolstoy, Remizov, Lidin, Pilnyak, Sokolov-Mikitov read their stories. Mayakovsky performed. Esenin, Marina Tsvetaeva, Andrei Bely, Pasternak, Khodasevich recited their poetry. Once I caught sight of Igor Severyanin, who had come from Estonia; he was as full of self-admiration as ever and read the same "poesies." A storm broke out at a lecture by the painter Puni; Archipenko, Altman, Shklovsky, Mayakovsky, Sternberg, Gabo, Lissitzky, and I argued furiously.[7]

The Russian colony flourished very briefly, then began to decline early in 1923, as inflation and political unrest took their toll. Some Russians, like Shklovsky and Bely, found exile intolerable and returned home at the comparatively low price of restricted creative activity. Others, like Gorky and

[7] Ilya Ehrenburg, *Memoirs: 1921–1941* (Cleveland and New York, 1963), p. 20. This book forms part of the memoirs entitled *Liudi, gody, zhizn'* [People, Years, Life], which Ehrenburg published in *Novyi mir* [The New World] between 1960 and 1965.

Tsvetaeva, lived in exile until the thirties, when they were drawn back to their native land to perish under tragic circumstances. Most of the refugees sought a new home elsewhere in Western Europe or in America. In *Zoo*, Shklovsky records the process of dissolution occurring, in equal measure but for different reasons, in both Russian and German Berlin—the grim mood recorded in the vitriolic paintings of George Grosz, whose book *Ecce Homo*, like *Zoo*, was published in Berlin during 1923.

Bewildered and penniless, driven from his native land and wretched in exile, Shklovsky compounded his difficulties by falling in love with a beautiful Russian girl named Elsa Triolet. Elsa was the daughter of a prominent Russian lawyer, Yury Kagan. Shortly after the revolution, she had married a Frenchman, André Triolet, and accompanied him to Tahiti. The marriage deteriorated, and the couple returned to Europe —Triolet to Paris, Elsa to Berlin.[8]

Elsa's sister, Lilya, to whom the first letter in *Zoo* is addressed, was well known at the time as wife of the formalist critic Osip Brik and mistress of the futurist poet Vladimir Mayakovsky. Mayakovsky had met Lilya while courting Elsa. In May 1915, he left Moscow to visit friends in Kuokkola, an artists' colony described by Shklovsky in Letter 4. While there, he made a trip to Petrograd to see Elsa, who was staying with her sister. It was a fateful encounter for everyone. Mayakovsky promptly fell in love with Lilya. Brik, who had recently completed law school, heard Mayakovsky declaim his poetry and offered to publish an edition of the poem "Oblako v shtanakh" (A Cloud in Pants). In this way, he

[8] *Ibid.*, pp. 23–24.

formed an association which soon led to a new career as publisher and critic.[9]

The fates of Mayakovsky and Shklovsky, old friends and colleagues, crisscrossed in a strange way at the end of 1922. Each was spurned by the sister of his choice. Both—Mayakovsky in Moscow, Shklovsky in Berlin—retired to lonely rooms and carved out of their despair remarkable works of literature about unrequited love and unregenerate bourgeois society—Mayakovsky his long poem "Pro eto" (About This), Shklovsky his *Zoo*. Ironically, Shklovsky, scornful of the bourgeois society which confounded him in Western Europe, spoke in *Zoo* of his nostalgia for the unspoiled Russia which Mayakovsky, in "Pro eto," was simultaneously denouncing for the resurgent bourgeois tendencies stimulated by NEP.

The two works have remarkable stylistic and thematic affinities. As futurists, both Shklovsky and Mayakovsky shared a predilection for hyperbolic images, which, in both works, results in personification of the telephone. Its thin wire may or may not enable them to make contact with the willful sisters. The tears profusely shed by each author coalesce into floods, one of which invades Elsa's apartment in the tenth letter; the other one bears Mayakovsky away on an ice floe. The floe eventually spirits him to the Berlin zoo, which he and Lilya had visited together, and he expresses the hope of becoming an attendant in his lady's zoo, should she ever acquire one.

[9] Viktor B. Shklovsky, *O Maiakovskom* [Mayakovsky] (3d ed., revised and included in *Zhili-byli*; Moscow, 1966), pp. 311–312. Shklovsky reviewed Mayakovsky's poem enthusiastically in the futurist journal *Vzial* [Took], which he, Mayakovsky, and Brik published in December 1915.

The personalities of Shklovsky and Mayakovsky stand very much in the foreground of all their work, and these two examples are no exception. The women in question are not cloaked in fictional garb, and the events are not recollected in tranquility. Shklovsky confuses his real self with the self coming to life between the covers of his book, while Mayakovsky converses at length with a projection of himself seven years younger.[10] Self-centered lyricism was not particularly welcome in the Russia of the early twenties, nor was it to be again until after the Stalinist era.

In August 1923—just before Shklovsky returned to Russia —the two men vacationed on Norderney, an island in the North Sea, where they commiserated over their difficulties with the two sisters. As Shklovsky wrote in his memoirs of Mayakovsky, "By the immense, alien sea, with the wind cutting our lips, our youth ended." [11]

For Elsa Triolet, the publication of Zoo had significant repercussions. Seven of the letters in the book were actually written by her, and these letters proved to be the debut of a distinguished literary career. When Shklovsky finished the book in January 1923, he sent the manuscript to Gorky. At the time, Gorky was laying the groundwork for a new journal, whose formation Shklovsky had suggested—a journal that would provide a forum not only for émigré Russians, but also for Soviet Russians, newly stymied by the stringent censorship instituted by the Bolshevik regime early in 1922. Gorky also intended to solicit contributions from the

[10] An annotated English version of "Pro eto" may be found in *Mayakovsky*, edited and translated by Herbert Marshall (New York, 1965), pp. 161-229.
[11] Shklovsky, *O Maiakovskom*, p. 381.

foremost Western European intellectuals; he hoped that the dissemination of their thoughts in Russia would mitigate the barbarism that had depressed and frightened him during the revolutionary years.

The poet Vladislav Khodasevich, a co-editor, chose the name *Beseda* (Colloquy) for the journal, of which seven issues were published between 1923 and 1925. Despite vague promises, the Soviet government never permitted the sale of this journal inside Russia, and Soviet authors almost immediately encountered insurmountable difficulties in sending their manuscripts outside Russia—all of which kept the journal from realizing the aims which Gorky intended and so infuriated him that he vowed not to contribute to any Soviet journals as long as the prohibition lasted (a vow soon forgotten).

The manuscript of *Zoo* reached Gorky at a moment when he was infuriated with Shklovsky. Gorky had just persuaded the poet Sergei Lvovich Rafalovich to join the staff of the prospective journal. One night, at the House of Arts, Shklovsky criticized one of Rafalovich's talks so savagely that Gorky feared the entire project was jeopardized. In a letter to Khodasevich, he gave vent to his annoyance:

16 February 1923

Dear Vladislav Felitsianovich,

Shklovsky writes:

"Via Epoch and Maksim, I've learned that you people in Saarow are after my head." [12] "In this Rafalovich incident, I'm certainly in the wrong."

[12] Epoch is the firm which published Gorky's *Beseda;* its owner, Solomon G. Kaplun (Sumsky), reported Gorky's displeasure to

"The reason for the incident is as follows: I had a temperature of 82.61 (a telephone number)." [13] "In short, I'm in love and desperately unhappy."

None of this consoles me in the slightest, nor does it change my opinion of the incident. Shklovsky thinks: "This whole business won't hurt the journal."

He sent three sketches. The first two I don't like at all, but "Cold Weather" I would like you to read. I need to know your opinion by Sunday. "Cold Weather," of course, requires major corrections and, here and there, cutting.

Warm greetings.

A. Peshkov [14]

The sketch of which Gorky speaks is the elegy to Khlebnikov, which became the fourth letter of *Zoo*. Gorky published this work, as well as three other letters (18, 26, and 27), in the first issue of *Beseda*. Not without malice, though, he observed that the best letters in the manuscript were those written by the woman, especially the one containing her impressions of Tahiti (21). He advised her to expand the letter into a book, and, throughout 1923, he met and

---

Shklovsky. Maksim is Gorky's son, Maksim Alekseevich Peshkov (1897–1934).

[13] The temperature is given according to the Réaumur scale, which registers the boiling point of water at 80 degrees.

[14] "Pis'ma Maksima Gor'kogo k V. F. Khodasevichu (1922–1925)" [Letters from Maksim Gorky to V. F. Khodasevich (1922–1925)], *Novyi zhurnal* [The New Review], no. 29 (1952), p. 206. An English translation of these letters, prepared by Hugh McLean, appeared in *Harvard Slavic Studies* (Cambridge, 1953), I, 280–334. The information in this introduction about *Beseda* comes from these letters and from the annotations prepared by Khodasevich.

corresponded with Elsa about this project.[15] The book,
entitled *Na Taiti* (On Tahiti), was completed and published
in 1925. Two other books, also written in Russian, followed:
Zemlianika (Wild Strawberries), 1926, and *Zashchitnyi svet*
(Protective Coloring), 1928. In 1928, Elsa married Louis
Aragon, and during the late thirties she began to write novels
in French. Her participation in the French Resistance resulted
in a book of stories entitled *Le premier accroc coûte deux
cents francs*, which was awarded the Prix Goncourt in 1944.
It is noteworthy that the French translation of *Zoo*, which
appeared in 1963, was published as part of a Russian series
sponsored by Elsa Triolet and Aragon. The translation was
done by Vladimir Pozner, once a member of the Serapion
Brothers; now, like Elsa, he is a famous French novelist.

The months which Shklovsky spent in Berlin were filled
with frenzied literary activity. During 1923, in addition to
A Sentimental Journey and *Zoo*, he published several articles
and two other books: *Khod konia* (Knight's Move), a
collection of theater criticism written in Russia before his
emigration, and *Literatura i kinematograf* (Literature and
Cinematography), his first major foray into film theory.

In the fall of 1923, his bizarre petition to the Central
Committee of the Communist Party (Letter 29) received a
favorable response, owing to the intercession of Gorky and
Mayakovsky, and Shklovsky returned to Russia. His return
seems to have been dictated by his chronic inability to adjust
to European life, though Nina Berberova suggests another

[15] *Letopis' zhizni i tvorchestva Maksima Gor'kogo* [Chronicle of
the Life and Work of Maksim Gorky], ed. B. V. Mikhailovsky,
L. I. Ponomarev, and V. R. Shcherbina (4 vols.; Moscow, 1958–1960),
III, 320–330.

possibility: that Shklovsky's wife was imprisoned after his defection and held as a hostage to ensure his return.[16] He did rejoin his wife, and they moved to Moscow, where their son Nikita was born in 1924.

II

Without you, fatal beauty! I should never have felt this unbearable contrast between the grandeur of my soul and the meanness of my fortune. I should have lived quietly and died content, without condescending to notice what rank I held on earth. But to have seen you and not be able to possess you, to adore you and be only an obscure man! To be loved and not be able to be happy! To live in the same places and not be able to live together! Oh Julie whom I cannot renounce! Oh destiny which I cannot surmount! What frightful struggles I undergo, and yet I can never overcome my desires nor rise above my powerlessness!

Jean-Jacques Rousseau
La Nouvelle Héloïse,
Part I, Letter 26

In his subtitle, *The Third Héloïse,* Shklovsky makes a pun on Elsa's name and establishes a parallel between his *Zoo* and Jean-Jacques Rousseau's interminable epistolary novel, *La Nouvelle Héloïse.* Both titles ultimately invoke the famous medieval Héloïse, ill-fated beloved of Abelard. Each of *Zoo's* literary models presents a young girl of good family who is seduced by her learned, but socially unacceptable, tutor, with whom the girl falls deeply in love. When the tryst is

[16] Nina Berberova, *The Italics Are Mine* (New York, 1969), pp. 197–198.

discovered, the young tutor is banished from the house, and the girl is placed in a convent (religious for Héloïse, secular for Julie). There, with only moderate success, she tries to forget her lover and develop her spiritual life. The tutors, unable to combat the social conventions arrayed against them, are forced into lives of celibacy. Both stories are preserved in a series of letters.[17]

This literary superstructure erected by Shklovsky is never explicitly mentioned in the body of the novel, but seems primarily designed to suggest ironic contrasts. All three heroes display unusual amounts of persistence, egocentricity, and self-pity in their love letters, but seem essentially dissimilar (one would not accuse Shklovsky of strong religious sentiments). The three heroines have even less in common, the fundamental discrepancy being that Elsa does not love Shklovsky—a fact which he laments, and avenges, with his *plume criminelle*. The passionate, stricken love letters of Héloïse and Julie differ notably from the indifferent, but tantalizing, letters of the self-indulgent Elsa.

At the same time, there are certain similarities between the novels of Rousseau and Shklovsky. For one thing, the ironic footnotes used by Rousseau have their counterpart in Shklovsky's epigraphs. There is also a parallel between

[17] For English versions, see *The Letters of Abelard and Heloise*, trans. by C. K. Scott Moncrieff (London, 1925) and *Julie, or the New Eloise*, trans. and abr. by Judith H. McDowell (University Park and London, 1968). It is an interesting coincidence that Laurence Sterne, whose novels *Sentimental Journey* and *Tristram Shandy* so deeply influenced Shklovsky, also wrote a book called *Journal to Eliza*, which is a highly autobiographical epistolary novel about unrequited love. The name Eliza even serves the pun made on the names Elsa (Elza in Russian) and Héloïse.

Saint-Preux's comments on Paris and Shklovsky's comments on Berlin. Both characters despise the elaborate social conventions—the preoccupation with appearances, the lack of sincerity—which they observe in those foreign capitals. In his book *Gamburgskii schet*, Shklovsky described the creative process which led to the construction of this bizarre epistolary novel:

Zoo was written by me in Berlin and originally conceived as a potboiler.

I wanted to present some character sketches of various people and embed in the book specimens of their work, i.e., Zinovy Grzhebin's trademark.

In this original, unwritten book were several character sketches that I later discarded; they were all very insulting. There was an article about the Changing Landmarks group and a character sketch of the owner of the Helikon publishing house; his name is Vishnyak.[18]

Even now, I'm restraining myself with difficulty from saying several unpleasant things about him.

But at the same time I had a completely different theme: I had to motivate the appearance of the unrelated pieces.

I introduced the theme of a prohibition against writing about love, and this prohibition let into the book autobiographical passages and the love theme. When I put the pieces of the finished product on the floor and sat down on the parquet to stick the book together, another book resulted—not the one which I had been making.

There are places in it that I revised; on the whole, I wrote the book in the heat of the moment; reading it aloud is impossible. The book is better than my purpose in writing it.[19]

[18] Abram Grigorevich Vishnyak (1895–1943).
[19] Viktor B. Shklovsky, "Retsenziia na etu knigu" [A Review of

Indeed, the book is essentially a series of impressionistic portraits, motivated by the author's persistent and abortive attempts to avoid the love theme. Since the traditional subject matter of the epistolary novel is love, preferably of the unrequited variety, Elsa's prohibition of this subject forces Shklovsky to renovate the genre by substituting unconventional material—not only the portraits, but also an elegy (Letter 4), urban landscapes (18), a dramatic fantasy (10), as well as essays on literary theory (especially 22) and criticism. In the course of the book, Shklovsky seeks to obey Elsa's edict by discussing literature. He ranges widely over both Russian and Western literature: Andersen, Boccaccio, Swift, Voltaire, Kipling, Tolstoy, Pushkin, Lermontov, folk and fairy tales; in all these literary forays, however, he finds only metaphors of his own plight, patterns which return him inexorably to the forbidden theme: his love for Elsa.

Elsa functions in the book as the heroine of a romance, but she is also, as the author explicitly states, a realized metaphor. She stands for the bourgeois values of effete Western Europe, which Shklovsky scornfully equates with creased pants and table manners. He prefers the less conventional values of Russia, its earthy provincialism and vitality, which he defiantly pits against European elegance and sophistication. On still another level of abstraction, he expresses that fear of Western technology which has disturbed Russian authors from Dostoevsky and Tolstoy to Solzhenitsyn. Especially in Letters 9 and 30, he warns that advances in science are separating man from nature and threatening to create a

---

This Book], *Gamburgskii schet* [Hamburg Account] (Leningrad, 1928), pp. 108–109.

machine-dominated civilization which will have no place for the individual.

The foregoing remarks explain the two cryptic subtitles of the book: *Letters Not about Love* and *The Third Héloïse*. As for the primary title, *Zoo*, it applies to the book in a variety of ways. The Berlin Tiergarten is located in what was then the Russian section of the city, and the Russians tended to take their strolls in its vicinity. On a less concrete level, Shklovsky saw painful parallels between the animals and their Russian counterparts. This parallel is carefully sustained throughout the novel—first of all, by the choice of epigraph: Velimir Khlebnikov's powerful poem "Menagerie" about the deterioration of caged animals. Letter 6, about the anthropoid ape in the Berlin zoo, reinforces this parallel, and echoes of it occur in the letter about Remizov (5), the elegy to Khlebnikov (4), and at the end of the letter about Hamburg (18).

The themes of love and captivity sounded in the titles securely bind the disparate segments of the book. Unity is also provided by the frequent Biblical parallels and by recurrent phrases. The twelve iron bridges mentioned in Letter 1, for example, recur in Letters 18 and 29, where they become emblematic of Shklovsky's tribulations. Other key phrases are "light-hearted," "six shirts," and "holding a fork properly." The pronunciation of Russian sibilants is a problem for both the blacks on Tahiti (Letter 21) and the Jews in the Ukraine (Letter 12), but the stakes are somewhat higher for the Jews: mispronunciation means death.

Throughout the book, Shklovsky comments frequently on his devices, especially in the ironic epigraphs which preface each letter. Here he ceases to be the frustrated lover and becomes the writer-technician, sitting at his table like a cobbler and shaping the raw material of his experience with a number of favorite tools. In this book, though, Shklovsky encounters real difficulties in observing the boundary between life and art, which, he had always insisted, divided two autonomous worlds. He can no longer separate his roles as literary technician and lover or Elsa's roles as realized metaphor and beloved. Evidence, both internal and external, suggests that Shklovsky was on the verge of a nervous breakdown when he wrote *Zoo*. The entire book is not so much a product scrupulously constructed as it is an exercise in sublimation, a fact most explicit in the elegy to Khlebnikov (Letter 4). Out of the torments of an unrequited love, Shklovsky has fashioned a book, and he suggests that a similar motivation has provided man with most of his cultural achievements.

The book that emerged from these torments departs radically from the traditional epistolary novel and from the novel tradition of nineteenth-century Russian literature. When *A Sentimental Journey* and *Zoo* appeared in 1923, the formalist critics Boris Eikhenbaum and Yury Tynyanov treated them as part of a promising trend that might create a new kind of documentary novel. Tynyanov, after surveying the Russian literary scene of the early twenties and finding it too indebted either to the West or to the nineteenth-century traditions of Russian literature, spoke approvingly of *Zoo* as a successful attempt to extend the borders of literature:

Shklovsky's *Zoo* "breaks new ground."

In the first place, of course, the letters do not give the impression of being personal letters—and in this sense they depart from both Rozanov's letters and Gorky's extracts, about which Shklovsky speaks in the novel. These are literary "letters," linked by literary images and many plot trajectories.

But what makes the book interesting? Why is prose rooted in images impossible for Bely and possible for Shklovsky? The book is interesting in that a single emotional core provides the basis for a novel, and a feuilleton, and a scholarly paper. We are not accustomed to reading a novel which is at the same time a scholarly paper. We are not accustomed to scholarship in "letters about love" or, for that matter, in "letters not about love." Our culture is built on a rigid differentiation between scholarship and art. Only in certain instances—very few at that—have these areas overlapped. Heine, for example, in his "Reisebilder," his "Parisian Letters" and, in particular, in his *History of Philosophy and Literature in Germany*, combined newspaper correspondence, portraits of a very personal nature, and the coarse salt of scholarly thought.

This novel, emotional to the point of sentimentality, is based on unusual material, which also "breaks new ground." [20]

Surely, though, *Zoo* is not literary in the sense that its distant relative, Dostoevsky's epistolary novel *Poor People*, is. True, the letters are self-conscious, perhaps even self-indulgent as most of the reviewers claimed, but they are highly personal despite the abundance of literary material. In fact, it could be argued that, in some ways, this idiosyncratic novel had forebears in the personal letter practiced by the Arzamas literary circle, to which Pushkin and Vyazemsky belonged. Their letters were written in the vernacular, with an intimate tone, and they had a mosaic quality, with snatches of poetry, word play, witticisms, and personal comments

[20] Yury Tynyanov, "Literaturnoe segodnia" [The Literary Today], *Russkii sovremennik* [The Russian Contemporary], I (1924), 305–306.

interspersed with literary observations. In that sense, Shklovsky's letters represent the revival and transformation of a genre canonized during the first quarter of the nineteenth century.[21]

At that time, Arzamas addressed itself directly to the problem of forging a new literary language to counter the stultified language of its remote predecessors and the poetic prose of its immediate predecessors. It sought to end the rigid dichotomy between conversational language and literary language. In the first quarter of the twentieth century, Opoiaz, the literary circle of the formalists, was involved in similar tasks—revolting against the style and structure of the Russian realistic novel and against the mellifluous prose of the symbolists. Both Tynyanov and Eikhenbaum saw *A Sentimental Journey* and *Zoo* as part of that revolt.

However one views the book—as a love story, an experimental epistolary novel, a sample of formalist prose, an evocation of Russian Berlin, a case study of Soviet censorship practices, or a story about the alienation and pain of exile—*Zoo* holds special meaning for Shklovsky, and he mentions it often in his work. In 1939, he celebrated its fifteenth birthday:

One of my books is fifteen years old: the novel *Letters Not about Love.*

If this novel were a boy, he would already be dreaming of trading his pellet gun for a rifle and riding a motorcycle.

[21] Especially relevant is Nikolai Stepanov's article "Druzheskoe pis'mo nachala XIX veka" [The Personal Letter at the Beginning of the XIX Century], *Russkaia proza: Sbornik statei* [Russian Prose: A Collection of Articles], ed. by B. Eikhenbaum and Yu. Tynyanov (Leningrad, 1926), pp. 74–101.

Actually, this book isn't quite that old.
If it were a human being, it would look younger.
But I am not as I was then and neither is she of whom I wrote.
Not as she was then.[22]

The bitterness and pain that inform the first edition continued to fade with the passage of time—from preface to preface. In the final preface, the author, now more than seventy years old, confronts once again that moment that has now receded nearly fifty years into the past. Alluding to the tribulations that the intervening years have brought, he contemplates that distant moment with a hard-won tranquility. Since that last preface, Elsa Triolet has died—in Paris, in 1970, at the age of seventy-three. Shklovsky still lives and writes books in Moscow.

RICHARD SHELDON
1971

[22] Viktor B. Shklovsky, *Dnevnik* [Diary] (Moscow, 1939), pp 4-5.

VIKTOR SHKLOVSKY

ZOO

or

Letters Not about Love

This book was written in the following way. Originally, I planned to do a series of essays on Russian Berlin; then it seemed a good idea to connect these essays with some sort of general theme. I took for my theme "Menagerie" ("Zoo"); thus the title of the book was born, but it failed to connect the pieces. Then came the idea of making some sort of epistolary novel out of them.

In an epistolary novel, the essential thing is motivation— precisely why should these people be writing to each other? The usual motivation is love and partings. I took the following variant of this motivation: the letters are being written by a man in love with a woman who has no time for him. Here I needed a new detail: since the basic material of the book had nothing to do with love, I introduced a prohibition against writing about love. What emerged I expressed in the subtitle "Letters Not about Love."

At this point, the book began to write itself. Something was needed to connect the material, that is, the love-lyrical line and the descriptive line. Submissive to the will of the material, I connected these things with a comparison: all the descriptions thus came out as metaphors for love.

°The woman—she to whom the letters are written—

acquired a certain configuration, that of a person from an alien culture, because there's no point in writing descriptive letters to a person of your own culture. I could have embedded a plot in the novel: for example, some descriptions of the hero's fate. But no one worships idols of his own making. I have the same attitude toward a plot of the usual type as a dentist to teeth.

I built the book on a dispute between people of two cultures; the events mentioned in the text serve only as material for the metaphors.°

This is a common device in erotic things, where real norms are repudiated and metaphoric norms affirmed. Cf. the *Esoteric Folk Tales*.[1]

Berlin
5 March 1923

Menagerie

O Garden, Zoological Garden!
Where the iron is like a father reminding brothers to be brothers and stopping their bloody grapple.
Where the Germans drink their beer.
And beauties sell their bodies.
Where the eagles sit, like an eternity finished with this day that still lacks evening.
Where the camel knows the secret of Buddhism and harbors the grimace of China.
Where the stag is pure terror, blooming like a massive rock.
Where the finery of the crowd is swank.
And the Germans bloom with health.
Where the swan is a replica of winter, despite the beak like an autumn thicket and the black gaze, somewhat guarded even for a swan.
Where the blue splendorial lowers a tail like Siberia seen from the Rock of Pavda [1] when the clouds throw a net of blue

over the gold of the fallage and the green of the forest, all of it tinted variously by the roughness of the land.

Where the monkeys, variously angry, flaunt the tips of their torsos.

Where the elephants, squirming as mountains squirm during an earthquake, beg a child for food, imparting an ancient sense to the truth: Give me food! I want to eat! and then kneel as if to supplicate.

Where the bears scramble deftly up and then look down, awaiting the orders of their keeper.

Where the bats hang suspended, like the heart of a modern Russian.

Where the breast of the falcon suggests the downy clouds that precede a storm.

Where the low-flying bird pulls in its wake the sunset and all the coals of its fire.

Where in the tiger's face, with its frame of white beard and the eyes of an elderly Moslem, we pay homage to the first Mohammedan and read the essence of Islam.

Where we begin to see the faiths as ebbing currents of waves whose surge is the various species.

And that the earth harbors animals in such multitude because each of them sees God in its own way. . . .

Where the cannon shot at noon compels the eagles to gaze skyward in expectation of a storm.

Where the eagles plummet from their lofty perches like idols toppled by an earthquake from temples and rooftops. . . .

Where after a brief rain, the ducks of a certain species cry out in unison as if offering a thanksgiving prayer to the deity of ducks—has it feet and beak?

Where the ash-silver guinea fowl have the aspect of professional beggars.

Where in the Malayan bear I refuse to recognize a fellow northerner and discover the Mongol there concealed.

Where the wolves convey compliance and devotion.

Where the parrots in their stifling habitat accost me as I enter with their choral salutations, "idiott, idiott!"

Where the fat and glistening walrus undulates, like a languid beauty, its black, slippery, fan-shaped foot, then leaps into the water; and when it slides once more onto the ramp, upon its massive, greasy body appear the spiny bristles and smooth brow peculiar to the head of Nietzsche.

Where the jaw of the white, black-eyed, exalted llama and the jaw of the flat-horned buffalo move evenly to the right and to the left, as does the life of a land with popular representation and a government responsible to the people— that paradise desired by so many!

Where the rhinoceros holds in its red-and-white eyes the unquenchable fury of a toppled tsar; he alone, of all the animals, regards mankind with the unconcealed disdain which tsars reserve for slave rebellions. In him lurks Ivan the Terrible.

Where the gulls, with long beaks and cold, blue eyes that seem ringed by spectacles, resemble international financiers, confirmation of which we find in the adroit way they filch the food thrown to the seals.

Where, remembering that Russians were wont to call their chieftains by the name of falcon, and remembering the keenness of Cossack and falcon eye alike, we begin to know who instructed the Russians in the art of war.

Where the elephants, their trumpet calls forgotten, make a

sound that seems to mourn their sad condition. Do they make such paltry sounds from deference to our own excessive paltriness? I do not know.

Where the animals lose their marvelous potentialities, like the *Lay of Igor's Host* embedded in a Book of Hours.[2]

Velimir Khlebnikov
(A Trap for Judges, I, 1909) [3]

I DEDICATE

ZOO

TO

ELSA TRIOLET

AND GIVE THIS BOOK THE NAME

The Third Héloïse

Letter One

Written by a woman in Berlin to her sister in Moscow. Her sister is very beautiful, with glistening eyes. The letter is offered as an introduction. Just listen to the calm voice!

I have by now adjusted to my new apartment. The landlady I suspect of being an ex-*fille de joie*, since she shows no signs of being spiteful or pesky. Hereabouts people speak only German and, however you come, you must make your way under twelve iron bridges. It is the sort of place you avoid if at all possible. My acquaintances from the Kurfürstendamm will not be casually dropping in!

The same men are still attached to me and show no signs of abandoning their posts. The third one has virtually pinned himself to me. I consider him my most outstanding decoration, though I am well aware of his amorous nature. He writes me one or two letters every day, brings them to me himself, then dutifully sits down beside me and waits for me to read them.

The first one still sends flowers, but is growing melancholy. The second one, the one to whom you imprudently consigned me, continues to insist on his love. In exchange, he demands that I come to him with all my troubles. Very shrewd, that one.

Taxi fares now cost 5000 times more than before.

Despite the peacefulness of my existence here, I miss London: the solitude, the measured life, the work from morning till night, the baths and the dances with attractive young men. Here I have learned to do without these things. And there is so much misery here that you can't put it out of your mind even for a minute.

Write soon about all your doings. I kiss you, my dear, most beautiful sister; thanks again for your love and affection.

Alya

7 February [1]

About love, jealousy, the telephone and the phases of love.
The letter ends with a remark about the way Russians walk.

Dear Alya,

I haven't seen you now for two days.

I call. The telephone squeals; I can tell that I've stepped on someone.

I finally reach you. You're busy in the afternoon, in the evening.

So I write another letter. I love you very much.

You are the city I live in; you are the name of the month and the day.

I float, salty and heavy with tears, barely keeping my head above water.

I seem to be sinking, but even there, underwater—where the phone doesn't ring and rumors don't reach, where it's impossible to meet you—I will go on loving you.

I love you, Alya, yet you force me to hang onto the running board of your life.

My hands are freezing.

I'm not jealous of people: I'm jealous of your time. It is impossible not to see you. So what can I do when there's no substitute for love?

You know nothing about the weight of things. All men

stand equal before you as before the Lord. So what can I possibly do? I love you very much.

At first, I was drawn to you as sleep draws the head of a train passenger toward his neighbor's shoulder.

Then I was mesmerized by you.

I know your mouth, your lips.

I have wound my whole life around the thought of you. I cannot believe that we have nothing in common; well, then—look in my direction.

I frightened you with my love; at the beginning, when I was still cheerful, you liked me better. That comes from Russia, my dear. We walk with a heavy tread. But in Russia I was strong; here I have begun to weep.

4 February

The second letter from Alya. In this one, Alya asks me not to write her about love. The letter is tired.

My dear, my own. Don't write to me about love. Don't. I'm very tired. As you yourself have said, I have come to the end of my tether. This daily grind pulls us apart. I do not love you and I will not love you. I fear your love; someday you will hurt me because of the way you love me now. Don't carry on so. I still feel we have much in common. Don't frighten me! As well as you know me, you still do all you can to frighten me, to repel me. Your love may be great, but it's far from joyful.

I need you; you know how to bring me out of myself.

Don't write me only about your love. Don't make wild scenes on the telephone. Don't rant and rave. You're managing to poison my days. I need freedom—I refuse to account for my actions to anyone!

Yet you demand of me all my time. Be light-hearted or else you'll fail at love. With each day, you grow more melancholy. You should go to a sanatorium, my dear.

I'm writing in bed, because yesterday I went dancing. Now I'm going to take a bath. Perhaps we'll see each other today.

Alya

5 February

Letter Four

About cold weather, the treachery of Peter, about Velimir Khlebnikov and his death.[1] About the inscription on his cross. Here too you will read: about Khlebnikov's love, about the cruelty of those who do not love, about nails, about the cup and about man's entire civilization, built on the way to love.

I'm not going to write about love. I'm going to write only about the weather.

The weather in Berlin is nice today.

The sky is blue, the sun higher than the houses. The sun looks right into Pension Marzahn, into Aikhenvald's room.[2]

I live on the other side of the apartment building.

Outdoors, it's nice and cool.

There was almost no snow in Berlin this year.

Today is February 5 . . . I'm still writing not about love.

I'm wearing a fall coat, but if it turned freezing cold, I would have to call it a winter coat.

I don't like the weather to be freezing or even cold.

Because of the cold, the Apostle Peter denied Christ. The night was cool and he walked up to the fire, but at the fire sat public opinion: the servants kept questioning Peter about Christ and Peter kept denying Him.

A cock was crowing.

The cold spells in Palestine are not severe. There it is certainly warmer than in Berlin.

If the weather that night had been warm, Peter would have remained in the darkness and the cock would have crowed for nothing, like all cocks, and in the gospel there would be no irony.

It's just as well that Christ wasn't crucified in Russia. Our climate is continental—severe cold and blizzards; the disciples of Christ would have flocked to the fires at the intersections and would have stood in line to deny Him.

Forgive me, Velimir Khlebnikov, for warming myself at the fire of alien editorial offices. For publishing my book, and not yours. Our climate, master, is continental.

Foxes have their holes, the prisoner is given a cot, the knife sleeps in its scabbard, but you had nowhere to lay your head.

In the utopia which you wrote for the journal *Took* was, among other things, the fantasy that every man should have the right to a room in any city.[3]

True, it said in the utopia that the room should be made of glass, but I think that Velimir would have settled for an ordinary one.

Khlebnikov has died and a certain dusty gentleman in *Literary Notes* has said something in flabby language about a "failure."[4]

In the cemetery, the artist Miturich wrote on the cross over the grave:

"VELIMIR KHLEBNIKOV
A PRESIDENT OF THE GLOBE."[5]

So the wanderer did find an abode, though not of glass.

It is doubtful, Velimir, that you would want to be resurrected to walk the earth again.

Yet on another cross was written:

"JESUS CHRIST
KING OF THE JEWS."

It was hard for you to wander through the steppes and to serve as a soldier, to guard warehouses at night and then, halfway a prisoner, to take part in the stormy performance of the imagists in Kharkov.[6]

Forgive us for yourself and for the others °whom we will kill.°

For warming ourselves at alien fires.

°The state is not responsible for the death of human beings. During the time of Christ, it did not understand the Aramaic language and it invariably fails to understand the language of humanity.

The Roman soldiers who pierced the hands of Christ are no more guilty than the nails.

All the same, those being crucified feel much pain.°

It was once thought that Khlebnikov failed to notice how he was living—the fact that his shirtsleeves were ripped clear to his shoulders, that his bed springs were not covered with a mattress, that the manuscripts which he used as pillow stuffing were lost. But on the verge of death, Khlebnikov remembered his manuscripts.

He died horribly. Of blood poisoning.

His bed was surrounded with flowers.

The only doctor in the vicinity was a woman, but he refused to let her touch him.

I remember the old days.

It was at Kuokkala—in the fall, when the nights are dark.[7]

During the winter I often met Khlebnikov at the house of a certain architect.

The house was splendid, the furniture Karelian birch, the

architect pale and intelligent (with a black beard). He had daughters.

Khlebnikov went there often. The architect read his verses and understood them. Khlebnikov looked like a sick bird. Sick birds don't like to be watched.

Like such a bird, he sat with drooping wings in an old frock coat and gazed at the architect's daughter.

He took her flowers and read her his things.

He renounced them all except "The God of Maidens." [8] He asked her how he ought to write.

It was at Kuokkala—in the fall.

Khlebnikov was living there, next door to Kulbin and Ivan Puni.[9]

I went there, found Khlebnikov and told him that the girl had married an architect, the father's assistant.

It was so simple.

Misfortune of this kind comes to many. Life is well ordered, like a *nécessaire*, but not all of us can find our places in it. Life tailors us for a certain person and laughs when we are drawn to someone unable to love us.

All this is simple—like postage stamps.

The waves in the gulf were also simple—Kuokkalesque. They are the same even now. The waves were like corrugated iron.[10] The clouds were fleecy. Khlebnikov said to me, "You've inflicted a wound, you know." I knew.

"Tell me, what do they need? What do women need from us? What do they want? I would have done anything. I would have written differently. Maybe fame is necessary?"

The sea was simple. People were sleeping in their summer cottages.

How could I respond to this Agony in the Garden?

Drink, friends—drink, great and small, from the bitter cup of love! No special qualifications required. Standing room only. And it is easy to be cruel—one need only not love. Love too understands neither Aramaic nor Russian. Love is like the nails used to pierce hands.

The stag uses its antlers in combat, the nightingale does not sing in vain, but our books avail us nothing. This wound will not heal.

All we have are the yellow walls of houses, lit by the sun; we have our books and we have man's entire civilization, built by us on the way to love.

And the precept to be light-hearted.

But what about all the pain?

Give everything a cosmic dimension, take your heart in your teeth, write a book.

But where is the one who loves me?

I dream of her and take her by the hand and call her by the name of Lusya, the blue-eyed captain of my life, and I fall fainting at her feet and I fall out of my dream.[11]

°O parting, O body broken, O blood spilled!°

Containing a description of Remizov, Aleksei Mikhailovich, and
his system of hauling water up to the fourth floor in bottles.
Here too are described the daily life and customs of the Grand
Order of Monkeys.[1] I have also inserted some theoretical
observations on the role of the personal element in the formation
of art.

I must tell you, Alya, that Asyka, tsar of the monkeys—
alias Aleksei Remizov—is in trouble again: he is being
evicted from his apartment.

They refuse to let the man be, though that is all he asks.

During the winter of 1919, Remizov was living in
Petersburg when a waterpipe in his house up and broke.

Anyone else would have been beside himself. But
Remizov collected bottles from all his acquaintances—small
medicine bottles, wine bottles and any others he could find.
He deployed them on the rug in his room, then took two at
a time and ran downstairs for water. With that system, it
took him a week to haul enough water for one day.

Most inconvenient, but . . . amusing!

Remizov's life—constructed to his specifications and
authenticated with his own tail—is most inconvenient, but
amusing.

He's short, with thick, close-cropped hair and a big

cowlick. He stoops, but his lips are as red as red can be. A pug nose, too, and the effect is calculated.

His whole passport is covered with monkey marks. Even before the waterpipe burst, Remizov had withdrawn from the society of human beings—he knew beforehand what sort of birds they are—and he went over to the great monkey folk.

The Order of Monkeys was devised by Remizov along the lines of Russian Freemasonry. Blok belonged. At the moment Kuzmin is the musician for the Grand and Free Chamber of Monkeys; and Grzhebin, that godfather of monkeys, holds, as in real life, the rank and title of acting prince—just for the duration.[2]

I too was taken into this monkey conspiracy. I gave myself the rank of "bobtailed monkey." I docked my tail with my own hands in Kherson before going off to join the Red Army.[3] Since you, Alya, are an acting foreigner and since your suitcases do not realize that their mistress was suckled by a Siberian woman, Stesha the ruddy, then I must also inform you that our monkey folk, made up of deserters from life, has a real tsar—a most worthy one.

Remizov has a wife—Serafima Pavlovna Remizova-Dovgello, very Russian, very russet and big. She is as incongruous in Berlin as a Negro in Moscow during the reign of Tsar Aleksei Mikhailovich, so fair and Russian is she.

Remizov is an Aleksei Mikhailovich, too. He once said to me: "I can no longer begin a novel: 'Ivan Ivanovich was sitting at the table.' "

Since I respect you, let me tell you a secret.

As a cow devours grass, so literary themes are devoured; devices fray and crumble.

A writer cannot be a ploughman: he is a nomad, constantly moving with his wife and herd to greener pastures.

Our grand monkey troop lives on the rooftops—like Kipling's cat, who walked "by his wild lone." [4]

You humans wear clothes and for you one day follows another. In killing—even more so in love—you're traditional. The monkey troop doesn't spend the night at the place where it dined and doesn't take its morning tea at the place where it slept. Monkeys are always on bivouac.

Our business is the creation of new things.[5] At the moment, Remizov wants to create a book with no plot, with no "man's fate" lodged at the base of the composition. He's writing one book made from bits and pieces—that's *Russia in Writ*, a book made from scraps of books; he's writing another one built on Rozanov's letters.[6]

It's impossible to write a book in the old way. Bely knows that, Rozanov knew it well, Gorky knows it when he's not thinking about syntheses °and Steinach;° and I, the bobtailed monkey, know it.[7]

We have introduced into our work the intimate, identified by first and last name, because of this same necessity for new material in art. Both Solomon Kaplun in Remizov's new story and Maria Fyodorovna Andreeva in his lament for Blok are dictated by literary form.[8]

The monkey troop does its duty. °Moving diagonally like a knight, I have intersected your life, Alya, and you know how that was and how it is; but you turn up in my book like Isaac at the fire built by Abraham. Still, you know,

Alya, that God so loved Abraham that he gave him an extra "a" in his name. Even to God, an extra sound seemed like a good present.

Do you know that, Alya?

However, you will not be the sacrifice: I am the substitute sacrifice, the lamb who caught his horns in the bushes.°

Remizov's room bristles with puppets and goblins.

Remizov sits there and hisses at everyone, "Hush! The landlady!" and raises a finger to his lips. He's not afraid of the landlady—it's a game.

Walking on sidewalks is hard for free monkeys—a way of life foreign to them. Human women are incomprehensible. The human routine is awful, meaningless, sluggish, inflexible.

°We play the fool in this world in order to be free.°

Routine we transform into anecdotes.

Between the world and ourselves, we build our own little menagerie worlds.

We want freedom.

Remizov lives a life based on the techniques of art.

I'll stop writing now. I have to run over to the Mierike bakery for a cake. Someone's coming to see me shortly, then I have to fetch the cake, then stop to see someone, then try to find some money, sell my book, talk to some young writers. Never mind, in the monkey economy, everything serves a purpose. The Tower of Babel makes more sense to us than Parliament, insults aimed at us can always be jotted down, "rose" and "snows" go together in our world because they rhyme.[9]

I will not give up my writer's trade or my free thoroughfare across the rooftops for a European suit, shined boots or a high rate of exchange—not even for Alya.

About misery and the captivity of our forefather. The letter ends with a tentative suggestion to begin publishing a newspaper for him.

The animals in the cages at the zoo look reasonably happy. They even bear young.

The baby lions are suckled by dogs, so they know nothing about their lofty origins.

Day and night, the hyenas scurry around in their cages like black marketeers.

All four of the hyena's paws are placed very close to its pelvis.

The adult lions languish.

The tigers pace behind the bars of their cages.

The elephants crinkle their hides.

The llamas are very pretty. Each one has warm wool clothing and a graceful head. Like you, Alya.

Everything is closed for the winter.

From the animals' point of view, it makes little difference.

The aquarium stays open.

In the blue water, lit by electricity and resembling soda pop, fish are swimming. Yet behind some of the glass panes, it's absolutely awful. A sapling sits there and quietly moves its white branches. Why did such misery have to be created in this world?

The anthropoid ape, instead of being sold, has been put on the top floor of the aquarium. You, Alya, are terribly busy, so terribly busy that I have a lot of time on my hands now. I visit the aquarium.

I have no use for the aquarium, but the zoo would have been useful for drawing parallels.

The ape, Alya, is about my height, but broader through the shoulders, stooped and long-armed. Sitting there in its cage, it doesn't look like an animal.

Despite the fur and the cauliflower nose, what I see behind those bars is a human being.

And that cage is no cage at all, but a prison.

There are two sets of bars, but I don't remember whether a guard walks between them or not. The ape languishes—it's a male—all day long. At three, he gets to eat. He eats from a plate. Afterward, he sometimes attends to his miserable simian needs. That's offensive and shameful.

You tend to think of him as a man, yet he's utterly without shame.

The rest of the time, the ape climbs around in his cage, looking apprehensively at the spectators. I doubt that we have the right to hold this distant relative of ours in prison without a trial.

And where is his consul?

Naturally, the ape languishes without his forest. People seem like evil spirits to him. All day long, this wretched foreigner languishes in his indoor zoo.

No one will even publish a newspaper for him.[1]

Letter Seven

About Grzhebin on canvas, about Grzhebin in the flesh.[1] *Since the letter is written in a penitent mood, the trademark of the Grzhebin Publishing House is affixed. Here too are several fleeting remarks about Jewry and about the attitude of the Jews toward Russia.*

What to write about! My whole life is a letter to you. We meet less and less often. I've come to understand so many simple words: yearn, perish, burn, but "yearn" (with the pronoun "I") is the most comprehensible word.

Writing about love is forbidden, so I'll write about Zinovy Grzhebin, the publisher. That ought to be sufficiently remote.

In Yury Annenkov's portrait of Zinovy Isaevich Grzhebin, the face is a soft pink color and looks downright delectable.[2]

In real life, Grzhebin is pastier.

In the portrait, the face is very fleshy; to be more precise, it resembles intestines bulging with food. In real life, Grzhebin is more tight and firm; he might well be compared to a blimp of the semirigid type. When I was not yet thirty and did not yet know loneliness and did not know that the Spree is narrower than the Neva and did not sit in the Pension Marzahn, whose landlady did not permit me to sing at night while I worked, and did not tremble at the sound of a telephone—when life had not yet slammed the door to Russia shut on my fingers, when I thought that I could break history on my knee, when I loved to run after streetcars . . .

> "When a poem was best of all
> Better even than a well-aimed ball"—[3]
> (something like that)

. . . I disliked Grzhebin immensely. I was then twenty-seven and twenty-eight and twenty-nine.

I thought Grzhebin cruel for having gulped down so much Russian literature.

Now, when I know that the Spree is thirty times narrower than the Neva, when I too am thirty, when I wait for the telephone to ring—though I've been told not to expect a call—when life has slammed the door on my fingers and history is too busy even to write letters, when I ride on streetcars without wanting to capsize them, when my feet lack the unseeing boots they once wore and I no longer know how to launch an offensive . . .

. . . now I know that Grzhebin is a valuable product. I don't want to ruin Grzhebin's credit rating, but I fervently believe that my book won't be read in a single bank.

Therefore I declare that Grzhebin is no businessman, nor is he stuffed either with the Russian literature gulped down by him or with dollars.

But, Alya, don't you know who Grzhebin is? Grzhebin's a publisher; he published the almanac *Sweetbriar*, he published *Pantheon* and now he seems to have the most important publishing house in Berlin.

In Russia, between 1918 and 1920, Grzhebin was buying

manuscripts hysterically. It was a disease—like nymphomania.

He was not publishing books then. And I frequently called on him in my unseeing boots and I shouted in a voice thirty times louder than any other voice in Berlin. And in the evening I drank tea at his place.

Don't think that I've grown thirty times narrower.

It's just that everything has changed.

I hereby give the following testimony: Grzhebin is no businessman.

Grzhebin is a Soviet-type bourgeois, complete with delirium and frenzy.

Now he publishes, publishes, publishes! The books come running, one after another; they want to run away to Russia, but are denied entry.

They all bear the trademark: ZINOVY GRZHEBIN.

Two hundred, three hundred, four hundred—soon there may be a thousand titles. The books pile on top of each other; pyramids are created and torrents, but they flow into Russia drop by drop.

Yet here in the middle of nowhere, in Berlin, this Soviet bourgeois raves on an international scale and continues to publish new books.

Books as such. Books for their own sake. Books to assert the name of his publishing house.

This is a passion for property, a passion for collecting around his name the greatest possible quantity of things. This incredible Soviet bourgeois responds to Soviet ration cards and numbers by throwing all his energy into the creation of a multitude of things that bear his name.

"Let them deny my books entry into Russia," says he— like a rejected suitor who ruins himself buying flowers to turn the room of his unresponsive beloved into a flower shop and who admires this absurdity.

An absurdity quite beautiful and persuasive. So Grzhebin, spurned by his beloved Russia and feeling that he has a right to live, keeps publishing, publishing, publishing.

Don't be surprised, Alya. We are all capable of raving— those of us who really live.

When you sell Grzhebin manuscripts, he drives a hard bargain, but more out of propriety than greed.

He wants to demonstrate to himself that he and his business are real.

Grzhebin's contracts are pseudo-real and, in that sense, relevant to the sphere of electrification in Russia.

Russia dislikes Jews.

All the same, though, Jews like Grzhebin are a good remedy for low blood pressure.

It's nice to see Grzhebin, with his appetite for the creation of things, in idle, skeptical Russian Berlin.

Letter Eight

With gratitude for the flowers that accompanied the letter about Grzhebin. This is the third letter from Alya.

Here I am, writing you a letter. Dear little Tatar, thank you for the flowers.

The whole room is saturated with their fragrance; I hated so to leave them that I didn't go to bed.

In this absurd room with its columns, its weapons and its stuffed owl, I feel at home.

The warmth, the smell, the peace and quiet belong to me.

I take them with me like a reflection in the mirror: When I leave, they leave. When I return, I look—and there they are.

I can hardly believe that they live in the mirror only through me.

Now I wish most of all that it were summer, that everything that has happened had not happened.

That I were young and strong.

Then, perhaps, of this cross between crocodile and child would remain only the child and I might be happy.

I'm no *femme fatale*. I'm Alya, pink and fluffy.

And that is that.

Alya

I kiss you, I sleep.

*About the three assignments given to me, about the question,
"Do you love me?"; about my corporal-of-the-guard, about how
Don Quixote is made;* [1] *then the letter switches to a speech about
a great Russian writer °and ends with a thought about my term
of service.°*

You gave me two assignments.

1) Not to call you. 2) Not to see you.

So now I'm a busy man.

There's still a third assignment: not to think of you. But
that one you overlooked.

You occasionally ask me if I love you.

Then I know that a sentry check is taking place. I reply
with all the diligence of a combat engineer who doesn't
know the garrison regulations very well:

"Post number three (not sure about the number);
location—at the telephone and in the streets from the
Gedächtniskirche to the bridges on Yorckstrasse, no farther.
Duties: to love, not to see, not to write—also to remember
how Don Quixote is made."

Don Quixote was made in prison—by accident. Cervantes
used his parody hero not only to caricature heroic deeds,
but also to deliver wise speeches. As corporal-of-the-guard,
Alya, you know yourself that one's letters have to be sent
somewhere. Don Quixote was given wisdom because there

was no one else in the novel who could be wise: the combination of wisdom and madness gave rise to the Don Quixote type.

I could say a lot more, but I see the slightly curved back and the tips of a small sable stole. You wear it that way to cover your throat.

I cannot desert; I cannot abandon my post.

The corporal-of-the-guard deserts without any qualms, pausing now and then to window-shop: looking through the glass at the slippers with pointed toes, at the long ladies' gloves, at the black silk shirts with white borders; looking intently—the way children look through the store window at a big, beautiful doll.

That's how I look at Alya.

The sun keeps rising higher and higher, as in Cervantes: "It would have melted the brains of the poor hidalgo if he had had any."

The sun stands over my head.

But I'm not afraid. I know how Don Quixote is made. He's made strong.

And he who is strongest will have a good laugh.

That will be the book.

And so while staying at my post by the telephone and touching it with my hand, the way a cat does with its paw when the milk's too hot, I'll just endow my Don Quixote with one more wise speech.

An important man promenades in Berlin. An acquaintance of mine. I have even accidentally switched mufflers with him a few times.

When he talks, his quiet voice changes quite unexpectedly to the wail of a shaman.

Once a shaman was brought to the Historical Museum in

Moscow. Having behind him the age-old culture of the shamans, this shaman wasn't bashful. He picked up a tambourine and cast his spells for some professors; he saw spirits and fell into an ecstasy.

Then he left for Siberia, to cast some spells there—only this time not for any professors.

In the man I'm discussing, ecstasy makes itself at home, but home is no summer cottage. And in one corner of the room, confined in a leather suitcase, lies a whirlwind.

His name is Andrei Bely.[2]

In real life, he is Boris Nikolaevich Bugaev.

Son of a professor.

In H. G. Wells' descriptions of life, you can see clearly how man is controlled by things.

Things have reshaped man—especially machines.

Nowadays man only knows how to start them, but then they continue running without any help. They run and run, and they crush man. In science the situation is extremely serious.

The certainties of reason and the certainties of nature have evaporated.

Once there was a top and a bottom, there was time, there was matter.

Now nothing is certain. Method reigns supreme.

Method was devised by man.

METHOD.

Method left home and started to live its own life.

The "food of the gods" was found, but we are not partaking.

Things—including the most complex of all things, the sciences—are overrunning the earth.

How do we put them to work for us?

And is it necessary?

We would be better off to build things useless and immense, but new.

In art, too, method leads a life of its own.

A man writing something big is like the driver whose 300-horsepower car dashes him against a wall—as if of its own volition. Drivers say that a car like that will "do you in."

Many times I have looked at Andrei Bely—Boris Bugaev —and thought how close he comes to being shy and how disarmingly amenable to everything he is.

Against his dark face, the gray hair seems almost white. His body is obviously strong. You can see how completely his arms fill his sleeves.

His eyes seem chiseled.[3]

Andrei Bely's method is very strong, incomprehensible even to him.

Andrei Bely started writing, I think, as a joke.

His "Symphony" was a joke.[4]

Words were placed next to other words, but the artist did not see them in the usual way. The joke disappeared; method emerged.

Finally he even found a name for the motivation.

The name was anthroposophia.[5]

Anthroposophia is a small thing created to tie up loose ends.

St. Isaac's Cathedral was built during the reign of Catherine the Great, but the arches were added during the time of Paul—in brick, with no attention paid to the proportions.

It was too much trouble.

And everyone wanted the cathedral finished.

Nowadays, a lot of people are enthusiastic about bending parallel lines and making the ends meet.

Anthroposophy is a word extremely unsuitable for the present day.

Lines of force these days do not intersect in us.

Nowadays, the construction of a new world is something we watch, not something we do.

In the stepped form of *Notes of an Eccentric*, where the reason of the poet-novelist wanders and seeks without seeing, as well as in the unsuccessful, but highly significant, *Kitten Letaev*, Andrei Bely creates several planes.[6] One is strong, almost real; the others move beneath it and seem like its shadows, thrown by many light sources, but it is these many planes that seem real, while the other one seems quite incidental. There is no reality of soul in the one or in the others: there is only method, a technique of deploying things in rows.

That is the wise speech with which I occupy myself while on duty.

I stand and, like any young soldier, I grow bored; I count the passers-by.

I console myself with tender words:

"Be patient. Think about something else, about other important and unhappy people. There is no harm in loving. And tomorrow perhaps the corporal-of-the-guard will come again."

°But how long will my term of guard duty be?

Interminable—I'm serving in an unofficial capacity.°

Letter Ten

About a certain flood in Berlin; in point of fact, the whole letter constitutes the realization of a metaphor; in this letter, the author attempts to be light-hearted and cheerful, but I know for sure that in the next letter he won't be able to carry it off.

What a wind, Alya! What a wind!

The wind is making the spires on the Gedächtniskirche sway.

When the wind blows like that in Petersburg, Alya, the water rises.

On those days, the chimes in the Petropavlovskaya Fortress are rung every quarter hour, but no one listens to them.

Everyone is too busy counting cannon shots.

The cannons shoot. One. One, two. One, two, three . . . eleven times.

A flood.

A warm wind, making its way toward St. Pete, pushes water up the Neva.

I'm glad. Yet the water keeps rising. And the wind is in the street, Alya—my spring wind, our Petersburg wind!

The water is rising.

It has flooded all Berlin; in the tunnel, a subway train has surfaced belly up, like a dead eel.

It has washed all the fish and crocodiles out of the aquarium. The crocodiles float without awakening, though they whimper because of the cold, but the water keeps mounting the steps.

Eleven feet. It's in your room, Alya. The water enters Alya's room quietly: on the steps, the water has no room to move around. But in Alya's room, the water encounters Alya's slippers. A play follows:

Slippers: Why have you come? Alya's asleep! (They love you, too.)

Water: (in a soft voice). Eleven feet, mesdames slippers! All Berlin has surfaced belly up; only thousand-mark notes are visible on the waves. We are the realizations of a metaphor. Tell Alya that she is once again on an island: her house is encircled and all because of Opoiaz.[1]

Slippers: Don't joke! Alya's asleep, you stupid high water! Alya's tired. Alya needs not flowers, but the smell of flowers. Alya needs from love only the smell of love and some tenderness. Never, never burden her °dear, tender° shoulders with anything more.

Water: O, dear mesdames, Alya's slippers. Eleven feet. The water is rising. The cannons are shooting. A warm wind is making its way here and keeping us from returning to the sea. The warm wind of true love. Eleven feet! The wind is so strong that the trees are lying on the ground.

Slippers: O, water, you have flowed into the wrong mill.[2] That's not nice. In matters of love, might does not make right.

Water: Not even a mighty love?

Slippers: No, not even a mighty love. Absolutely not! Don't torment her with your might. She doesn't even need life. She, my Alya, loves the dance because it's the shadow of love. Love Alya, but not your love for her.

And the water departs, awkwardly dragging across the floor a briefcase full of page proofs. As the water is going out the door, the slippers turn to one another and say:
"Oh, spare me these literary types!"
The slippers aren't malicious, but they are a twosome, and two women standing next to each other for such a long time can't help gossiping.
This letter I wrote and rewrote. Now, in your honor, Alya, I'll rewrite it all over again.
So God registered a rainbow in honor of the "Universal Deluge."

Letter Eleven

*About a woman shopping for a dress and about things equipped
with hands. Here is noted a certain misunderstanding about
tuxedos. But the main content of the letter is a story about how
a Kerensky banknote once popped into Pyotr Bogatyryov's hat,
how he managed to keep from weeping in Moscow and how he
began weeping in a Prague restaurant.*[1]

So I'm writing about an alien culture and an alien woman.

The woman is perhaps not totally alien.

I'm not complaining about you, Alya. But you are an
utter woman.

You say, "When you've wanted a certain dress for a
long time, it doesn't pay to buy it—you've memorized it to
tatters."

Without fail, though, the woman in question flirts with
the things in the store: she likes everything.

That's the European mentality.

Naturally, a thing has only itself to blame if it doesn't
know how to become loved.

Especially things equipped with hands.

But every soldier carries his defeat in his pack.

When killed on the battlefield, he merely acknowledges
his destiny.

We don't know how to be light-hearted.

The wife of the eminent surgeon Ivan Grekov took offense at me and Misha Slonimsky because we went to a party at her place in our boots and field jackets.[2] Everyone else was wearing tuxedos.

The reason for our rudeness was simple: their tuxedos were all old. A tuxedo lasts a long time and can survive a revolution.

But we had never worn tuxedos. First we wore our high-school and university coats, then soldiers' overcoats and then field jackets made from those overcoats.

We have known no other way of life than that of war and revolution. It may be harming us, but we cannot escape it.

The store mentality is foreign to us. We're used to few things; anything extra was given away or sold. Our wives wore sacks and their feet grew a size larger.

Europe is destroying us. It upsets us and we take everything seriously. You know Pyotr Bogatyryov. He's short and blond, with blue eyes and short pants. Pants seem especially short on short-legged men. Bogatyryov's shoes are always unlaced.

When he walks down the street, either he goes slowly, on tiptoes, or else he runs diagonally, like a rabbit. He doesn't talk: he bellows.

This character was born into the family of a shop foreman, in the village of Pokrovskoe on the Volga. Since he was good at reciting poetry, he got into a gymnasium. He graduated. He entered the university as a budding philologist and took up the theory of anecdotes.

Bogatyryov writes a lot and then loses the manuscripts.

In hungry Moscow, Bogatyryov had no idea that he was

living badly. He lived and wrote—some good things and some potboilers, like everybody else, but without malice.

One evening after the theater, Bogatyryov was walking home through the snowdrifts of Moscow. He got tired, took off his hat and began wiping his brow.

All of a sudden, into his hat popped a Kerensky banknote.

He looked around and saw a military personnel receding into the distance.

He ran after him. "Comrade, I don't need it!"

"Now don't be embarrassed. Take it."

Bogatyryov didn't take it, but he didn't take offense, either.

No one can insult us, because we work.[3]

No one can make us ridiculous, because we know our value.

But our love is the love of men who have never worn tuxedos and it makes no sense to any woman who has not borne with us the weight of our lives.

While Bogatyryov was giving lectures at various institutes and collecting revolutionary folklore, he made friends with °my friend and brother° Roman Jakobson.[4]

When Roman left for Prague, he wrote for Bogatyryov to come.

Bogatyryov went, with his pants short, his shoes unlaced and his suitcase filled with manuscripts and torn papers—everything so jumbled that it was impossible to tell research notes from pants.

Bogatyryov bought some sugar, kept it in his pockets and ate it—in short, attempted to maintain a Russian way of life.

But Roman, with his narrow feet and his red, blue-eyed head, loved Europe.

°He takes after you, Alya.°

Roman took Bogatyryov to a restaurant: Pyotr sat there, amid clean walls, assorted foods, wines and women. He began to weep.

It was more than he could bear. This European way of life defrosts us.

We have no use for it. However, everything is useful for drawing parallels.

°Bogatyryov didn't stay with Roman: he started looking for a Russian climate.

A place was found for him. He was offered a spot in a concentration camp for Russians returning to their native land.

There live Cossacks and officers; they dislike Europe immensely, Alya.

They sing Russian ditties and they know nothing but war.

Pyotr lived peacefully in the camp. It was a familiar way of life.° He wrote a book called *The Czech Puppet Theater and the Russian Folk Theater,* then he came to Berlin and I published his book because you're so busy that I have a lot of time on my hands—and also because I know how to work.[5]

As for Bogatyryov, he has picked up three new suits and he runs around in still a fourth, which is evidently some sort of national costume—Muscovite.

Now he finds even the Prager Diele bearable.[6]

He had begun to weep in Prague not out of sentimentality, but the way windows weep in a room heated for the first time in many weeks.

Letter Twelve

Written, it would seem, in response to a comment apparently made by telephone, since the dossier contains nothing in writing along these lines; the comment had to do with table manners. Also contained in the letter is a denial of the assertion that pants absolutely must be creased. The letter is liberally garnished with Biblical parallels.

So help me, Alya, pants don't have to be creased!

Pants are worn to thwart the cold.

Ask the Serapions.[1]

As for hunching over one's food, maybe that ought to be avoided.

You complain about our table manners.

We hunch down over our plates to minimize the transportation problem.

We will no doubt continue to surprise you—and you us.

A great deal surprises me about this country, where pants have to be creased in front. Poor people put their pants under the mattress overnight.

In Russian literature, this method is well known; it's used— in Kuprin—by professional beggars of noble origin.[2]

This whole European way of life provokes me!

Just as Levin was provoked (*Anna Karenina*) when he noticed how fruit was being canned in his house—not his way, but the way it had always been done in Kitty's family.[3]

When Judge Gideon was gathering a guerrilla band for an attack on the Philistines, he first of all sent home all the family men.

Then the Angel of the Lord commanded him to lead all the remaining warriors to the river and to take into battle only those who drank water from the palm of their hands, and not those who hunched over the water and lapped it like dogs.[4]

Are we, by any chance, bad warriors?

Well, when everything collapses—and that will be soon—we will leave two by two, with our rifles on our shoulders, with cartridges in the pockets of our pants (not creased); we will leave, firing at the cavalry from behind fences; we will head back to Russia, perhaps to the Urals, there to build a New Troy.[5]

But it is preferable not to hunch over one's plate.

Terrible is the judgment of Gideon the judge! What if he refuses to take us into his army!

The Bible repeats itself in curious ways.

Once the Jews defeated the Philistines, who fled, fleeing two by two, to seek safety on the other side of the river.

The Jews set out patrols at the crossing.

On that occasion, it was difficult to distinguish a Philistine from a Jew: both were, in all likelihood, naked.

The patrol would ask those coming across, "Say the word 'shibboleth.'"

But the Philistines couldn't say "sh"; they said "sibboleth."

Then they were killed.[6]

In the Ukraine, I once ran across a Jewish boy. He couldn't look at corn without trembling.

He told me this:

When the killing was going on in the Ukraine, it was frequently necessary to check whether the person being killed was a Jew.

They would tell him, "Say 'kukuruza.'"

The Jew would say "kukuruzha."

He was killed.[7]

Letter Thirteen

Written between six and ten a.m. That excess time made the letter long. It has three parts. The only important thing in it is the observation that the women in a certain Berlin Nachtlokal know how to hold a fork.

SIX A.M.

Outside the window, in Kaiserallee, it's still dark.

I have your permission to telephone at 10:30.

Four and a half hours, then another twenty empty hours, and between them your voice.

My room is hateful to me. Not dear to me is my writing desk, on which I write letters only to you.

Here I sit, as much in love as any telegraph operator.

It would be nice to get a guitar and sing:

> You, at least, please speak to me,
> O friend with seven strings.
> Such anguish fills my soul, you see,
> And tonight the moonlight stings.[1]

I have to write a potboiler—a film advertising motorcycles.

Thoughts about you, motorcycles and automobiles swirl in my head.

I will write a letter. The film can wait.

I write you every night, then I tear up the letter and

throw it in the wastebasket. The letters revive, mend and I write them again. You receive everything I've written.

In your wastebasket for broken toys is the man who gave you flowers for a farewell present; you called and thanked him. In the same receptacle is the man who gave you the amber amulet and the one from whom you gladly took a small woman's purse woven of steel mesh.

Your routine is always the same: a jolly meeting, flowers, then the love of the man, which always lags behind, like the suction of fresh gas into the cylinder of an automobile.

A man begins to love on the day after he has said, "I love you."

Therefore those words should not be said.

The love keeps growing, the man's ardor increases, but by then you have lost interest.

When this lack of synchronization happens in an engine, the car backfires.

Only I, torn and shredded like a letter, keep climbing out of the wastebasket for your broken toys. I will survive dozens more of your passing fancies; every day you tear me up and every night I revive, like the letters.

It's not even morning yet and I'm already standing guard.

The window facing the street is open.

The automobiles have awakened, too, or else they never went to bed.

"Al, Al, El," they shout—trying to pronounce your name.

I sit here with my malady; I think about you, about automobiles. (The combination helps.)

You have turned my life the way a worm screw turns a rack.

A rack, however, is unable to turn a wheel. In technical

language this is called a stationary transmission. °Stationary is my fate.°

Only time, as they sing in the Odessa thieves' song devised by Livshits, belongs to me.[2] I can divide the waiting into hours and minutes; I can count them. I wait and wait. Too bad there's no guitar around. I will not hear Alya's voice soon.

What should I wait for, then? I'll wait for the sun. The sun will rise about eight. It will illuminate Kaiserallee and the street will look like Kamennoostrovsky Prospekt.

On Kamennoostrovsky in Petersburg stood the gymnasium from which I graduated.

It was some year or other—1913, I guess.[3] We were the graduating seniors of the gymnasium. We wanted badly to graduate and to roll out into the street, turning cartwheels like wooden hoops.

The air was full of wishes; they floated over Kamennoostrovsky like feathers, like wings. The clouds were feathery.

We were in a hurry to get life in our clutches. But we lacked the necessary words; we thought you could grasp a woman like a thing—by the handle.

°We slept with many of them—mechanically, the way a man planes boards.° With hot hands, or cold, we grabbed at life. We wanted to try various categories of love. During our gymnasium parties, we would cut the electric wires; those who caught a serious disease shot themselves willingly, as if wanting to try one more category. We were accustomed to these deaths. We were *morituri*, which means "those who are about to die." °When we were about to graduate, a whole crowd of us got a prostitute, undressed her, fitted her with a candle and played cards on her back. Afterward, we paid her well and urged her not to be too offended.°

The *morituri* had just wanted to try one more category.

No, it's better to sit in a room, to be awake at six A.M., and to go to the marketplace for flowers at seven. It's better to live all of life to the sound of a guitar.

Strange are the dives in Berlin. Once I landed in what the Germans call a *Nachtlokal*. It was an ordinary room, with photographs on the walls. A strong smell came from the kitchen. A piano was playing in the background. A violinist was sawing on a strange violin with the sounding boards cut completely out. The clientele was dead drunk. Out strolled a naked woman in black stockings; she danced, awkwardly moving her arms. Then out walked another—without stockings.

I had no idea who else was sitting in the room. The violinist went from table to table, collecting money. He went up to a glumly drunk man sitting in the corner and the man said something to him.

The violinist raised his mutilated violin and in the air hung ever so thinly "God Save the Tsar."

It had been a long time since I heard that particular anthem.

The woman had finished her dance and donned a ready-made, fairly stylish dress; she was sitting at the next table, eating something.

"See, she even knows how to hold a knife," said Bogatyryov to me. Table manners were a popular topic with us. We decided to head for home. In the anteroom, a woman was handing out coats. When I gave her the number, I looked closely at her face. It was the woman who had just been dancing in stockings. Everything was arranged very portably and probably kept in the family. As for debauchery, there was, in all likelihood, none. There are people with words and people without words. People with words persist and, believe me, I have had a happy life.

Without the word, one will never get to the bottom of anything.

The sky is growing light, but that is no reason to stop writing. Time belongs to me. Livshits is right.

My sleepless letter has unraveled. Let's knit it together before tearing it to pieces.

In one of the Bogomils' legends, God wants to get some sand from the bottom of the sea.[4]

But God is reluctant to get wet, so He sends the devil and bids him say, when he takes the sand, "It is not I who take, but God."

To the very bottom dived the devil, to the bottom he whirled; he seized the sand and he said, "It is not God who takes, but I."

A proud devil.

The sand was not given. The devil surfaced, blue.

Once again did God send him into the water.

To the bottom swam the devil, and, scraping the sand with his talons, he said: "It is not God who takes, but I."

The sand was not given. The devil surfaced, gasping for breath. For the third time did God send him into the water.

In a folk tale, everything is done three times.

The devil saw that he was getting nowhere.

He hated to spoil the plot. He began weeping, I imagine, and he dived. He swam to the bottom and said, "It is not I who take, but God." He took the sand and he surfaced. And out of the sand taken from the bottom by the devil, at God's behest, God created man.

I don't feel like writing anymore. I have no use for letters; I have no use for a guitar. And I don't care one way or the other whether my love is like a stationary transmission. °I just don't care. I know one thing: you won't even put my letter in the basket on the right side of your table.°

Written to Russia; it's clear from the letter that the author is suffering from an idée fixe. _The letter talks about how hard it is, even after Einstein's discovery, to live without taking up either time or space. The letter ends with an expression of indignation regarding the incorrect usage of the pronoun "we" in Berlin._

Dear friends, why do you write me so infrequently?

Can it be that you have extracted me from your hearts?

Save me from the shadow people, from those who have doffed their harnesses, from corrosion, from the whole life that tells me one thing:

"Go on living, but don't take up either my time or my space." And goes on to say:

"Here's the day and here's the night; live in the intervals between them. But don't come around in the morning or evening."

My friends, brothers! How wrong it is that I am here!

Go, all of you, into the street, into Nevsky Prospekt and plead, demand that I be allowed to return.

To avoid any unpleasantness, you might want to go down Nevsky in a streetcar.

But hold your ground, friends.

I am bound to Berlin, but if I were told, "You can return,"

I swear by Opoiaz that I would go home without looking back, without taking my manuscripts. Without making a telephone call.

°I've been forbidden to telephone.°

What are you writing these days?

Have they fixed the pothole in the pavement on Morskaya Street across from the "House of Arts"? [1]

Better to drop dead in that pothole and repair the road for Russian trucks than to live uselessly.

Are there many automobiles in Petersburg?

Are you getting things published?

We're publishing quite a bit.

But here "we" is a funny word.

A certain woman called me on the telephone. I was sick. We talked a while. I said I was staying home.

And she told me, as she was hanging up:

"We're going to the theater today."

Since I had just been talking to her, I didn't understand: "Who is this 'we'? I'm sick."

"You have it all wrong! 'We' is I and somebody else."

In Russia, "we" is stronger.

Letter Fifteen

About Ivan Puni and his wife, Ksana Boguslavskaya.[1] About how a painter loves and how one ought to love a painter, about Puni's friends and about how books and paintings are born. The content of the letter is didactic.

How hard it is—even in letters, even through the black paper mask I make you wear, even in dreams—how hard it is for me to see your face.

Woman with no vocation, how do you spend your time? Is it really nice, Alya, to take bread from people and give it to dogs?

There are two kinds of dogs: those who beg and those who don't.

For me, Berlin is encircled by your name.

No news of the world gets through.

And Ksana Boguslavskaya-Puni is down with diphtheria.

Poor girl, poor painter, poor painter's wife! I looked attentively at her and her husband until I met you.

I have known Vanya Puni for ten years now—since "Streetcar V." [2] (That's the name of an exhibition.)

He takes no notice whatsoever of his surroundings, though he is not in love; he apparently loves no one and can get along without people; he receives them absent-mindedly.

He has one sad love—his paintings. Just as I have failed to

love you joyfully, so Puni, all his life, has loved art joylessly.

You will never be fair to me, because you have no vocation and no love, and if you have any sense of morality, it will not protect someone as strong as you.

Why should you be fair when you can tell me anytime, "I didn't ask you to love me," and then put me aside?

Don't be surprised that I cry out even when you're not hurting me.

It was you who taught me the principle of relativity. Imagine Gulliver among the giants: a female giant is holding him in her hand—just barely, almost not holding him at all; she has simply forgotten to let him go, but will release him at any moment; poor Gulliver cries out in terror and picks up the telephone to say—don't drop me!

Ivan Puni is in love with his paintings; he watches the fate of art sadly, because for him nothing is simple and he cannot be certain of gaining the approbation of tomorrow.

One night I went to see him with Roman Jakobson, Carl Einstein,[3] Bogatyryov and someone else.

It was one or two A.M.; I don't remember which. Puni was still working in his studio. On the floor, on the chairs, on the bed lay tubes of paint.

He received us without joy and without consternation, as if we were passengers and his room a railroad car.

We talked to each other about many things, all of them bitter. We ate potatoes as they came off the coals. Puni gave us some bacon and cooked the potatoes, but took no notice of us. He was looking sadly and attentively at a painting.

And once I saw him laughing hard at one of his paintings: a design can amuse him as much as a witticism.

Ksana Boguslavskaya is the painter's wife and a painter in

her own right. Not a bad painter, either, though somewhat saccharine. In fact, probably a good painter, because the saccharine quality is intentional—a device. It has nothing to do with tears.

The most wonderful thing about her is that she is enamored of her husband's paintings. She jealously defends one variant against another and gets excited about what will come next.

But a painter needs bread; to get it, he must do potboilers. His shoulders physically ache from doing them. Real paintings don't sell—or, in any case, a painter has to wait a long, long time before he's recognized. We often jokingly refer to the Puni household as "The Holy Family," and sometimes *G. m. b. H.*[4] But the family, by the way, really is holy: if you translate the language of Berlin into some ancient tongue, you get the flight into Egypt, with Ksana as Joseph, Puni as the mother and a painting as the infant.

Life is hard for every man who loves a woman or his trade.

Puni is visited by friends: Frieg, a blond German with a beautiful wife; a Latvian named Karl Zalitt, as boisterous as a fourth-century African Christian; Arnold Dserkahl, who looks like a Swede—huge, reticent, well dressed, strong and incomprehensible to me. Another frequent visitor is Rudi Behling, a Frenchified German, a sculptor built like a grasshopper: the expressionistic mannequins in the various shop windows of Berlin were made from his models.

All these people are calm and quiet when they look at the paintings. But Ksana gazes at the canvases with eyes full of love. °I don't think Puni noticed the revolution and war° —he was working hard the whole time.

Paintings devour him. It is so hard to work!

These things are born like children.

Conceived in joy—joy, not shame—then carried with difficulty and delivered in pain, to live forever after in bitterness.

Letter Sixteen

From Alya again, her fourth, about how she doesn't want anything.

My dear, I'm sitting on the divan you don't like and thinking how very nice to be warm, comfortable and in no pain.

All my things have the reserved and reticent look of well-bred people.

The flowers come right out and say—we know, but we're not telling—and what they know, no one knows.

The pile of books which I can read and don't read, the telephone into which I can speak and don't speak, the piano on which I can play and don't play, the people whom I can see and don't see and you, whom I should love and don't love.

Yet without the books, without the flowers, without the piano, without you, my own, my dear, I would cry.

At this moment, I'm all curled up and, like a true woman of the East, I'm meditating.

I watch the stupid pattern repeated on the stove; I absurdly mimic the teapot—one hand on my hip, the other bent like a spout—and I rejoice at the likeness; I scrutinize a white azalea that, for some reason, is trembling.

I let my mind wander.

My dear, I'm not trying to hurt you; please don't think I'm trying to hurt you. I feel that you're beginning to think me unduly self-confident. No, I know I'm good for nothing; no need to insist on that.

My purchases lie unopened on the table.

A very short time ago, I would have come home and undressed to try on this new nightgown, but now it lies there, wrapped in paper.

Alya

Letter Seventeen

In which Alya's comment about ocean liners is developed and dancing on deck is mentioned—also automobiles, Boris Pasternak, the Moscow Press Club and our destiny.[1]

You did a good job of telling me about the ocean liner. °I'm a regular repository for your words.° You said that on such a ship, one has a constant sense of being pulled. Not really movement, but, more precisely, propulsion—motion forward and its potential. That makes sense to anyone who drives. Every car pulls in its own way. A good car presses very pleasantly against your back as if pushing with one hand. The main attraction of a good car is the quality of its propulsion, the quality of its acceleration. It has the effect of a singer's crescendo. The voice-propulsion of the Fiat amplifies very pleasantly. You press the accelerator and the car, wild with enthusiasm, carries you forward. In some cars, the acceleration is good but jerky. I especially remember a sixty-horsepower Mitchell of that sort. All your sensations are different in an automobile: you feel PROPULSION and peace of mind, PROPULSION and anxiety. But everything you feel is conditioned by the sensation of movement pressing against you.

I have never seen an ocean liner. But I love and understand it. It must be very nice to dance on a floor that moves, to exchange kisses and to think, with the thoughts lagging slightly behind the movement, like the heart in a descending elevator.

It must be like thinking to music, only better. Like the conversation of Dolokhov (*War and Peace*) to the singing of "Ah, you bower, my bower!" when he tried unsuccessfully to pick a fight with his comrade.[2] A new world is being born, new sensations; not everyone is aware of them yet. Our country is being pulled somewhere by a tugboat.

Your sister happened to be sitting in the Moscow Press Club. It was probably cold; there were a lot of newspaper people around. She, however, was sitting with Pasternak, Boris. He spoke in his usual way—hurling a dense throng of words this way and that, but the most important thing remained unsaid. The most important word.

But Pasternak himself was so fine that I'm going to describe him right now. His head has the form of an egg-shaped rock—compact and solid; his chest is broad, eyes brown. Marina Tsvetaeva says that Pasternak resembles both an Arab and his horse.[3] Pasternak is always straining in some direction, but without hysteria: he pulls like a strong and fiery horse. He trots, but he wants to gallop, throwing his legs far forward. After numerous incomprehensible words, Pasternak said to your sister:

"You know, we're like people on a ship."

This °important and happy° man, standing among people wearing overcoats and munching sandwiches at the counter in the Press Club (which is both funny and sad, albeit a trivial sadness), was feeling the propulsion of history. He feels movement; his poems are remarkable for their propulsion: the lines bend; they do not align themselves like steel bars; they collide like the cars of a suddenly braked train. Good poems. °A happy man. He will never be embittered. He will surely be loved, pampered and great to the end of his life.°

Pasternak is uneasy in Berlin. He's a man of Western culture—at least, he understands it: he lived at one time in Germany. Now he has a fine young wife with him, yet he's still very uneasy. It seems to me that he feels among us an absence of propulsion—and I say this not merely to make the letter circular.[4] We are refugees. No, not refugees but fugitives—and now squatters.

For the time being, anyway.

Russian Berlin is going nowhere. It has no destiny.

No propulsion.

How clearly I feel this! Perhaps, Alya, that's why you're attracted to foreigners—Englishmen, Americans; perhaps it's dreary for you with us because you too feel this. Foreigners have a mechanical propulsion—the propulsion of an ocean liner, on whose deck it's nice to dance the shimmy. We are losing our women. It is time to start thinking of ourselves. We men are internal-combustion engines; hauling barges is our business. °The revolution has lost its propulsion.° The deck of the ship remains, but we have no ballroom slippers.

Letter Eighteen

*About inevitability and the predictability of the denouement.
While waiting for the denouement, this correspondent writes
first about Hamburg, then about gray-striped Dresden and finally
about Berlin, the city of ready-made houses; the letter goes on
about the ring through which pass all the author's thoughts,
about his nightly trip under the twelve iron bridges and about a
chance encounter. Also about the fact that words are futile.*

I am completely bewildered, Alya! This is the problem:
I'm writing letters to you and, at the same time, I'm
writing a book. And what's in the book and what's in life
have gotten hopelessly jumbled. You recall that I wrote
you about Andrei Bely and about method. Love has its
own methods, its own logic—set moves established without
consulting either me or us. I pronounced the word "love"
and set the whole thing in motion. The game began. And
I no longer know where love ends and the book begins.
The game is underway. After a hundred pages or so, I
will be checkmated. The beginning is already played out.
No one can change the denouement.

Tragic endings—at the very least, a broken heart—are
inevitable in an epistolary novel.

Meanwhile, though, just for my own benefit, I'll tell
about the setting in which the action is taking place.

Berlin is hard to describe.

To describe Hamburg, you can always say something about the seagulls over the canals, about the shops, about the houses leaning over the canals, about everything customarily depicted.

When you enter the free port of the city of Hamburg, the locks part like a curtain. A theatrical effect. A vast watery field, cranes bowing, black buckets filling their gullets with coal from the ships. Their jaws snap open in both directions at once—like crocodiles' jaws. Tall, fretted hoists of the port type—as high as the shot from a "Nagant." [1] Floating elevators which can suck out as much as 20,000 bushels of grain a day.

I might swim up to one of those suckers and say: "Dear comrade, please suck out of me the 20,000 devils of love which are ensconced in my soul."

Or I might ask the biggest crane of all to lift me by the scruff of my neck and show me the lock-ridden Elbe, the heaps of iron and the boats, beside which cars are but fleas. And I might ask the steam shovel to say to me: "Look, you sentimental pup, at the iron standing on its hind legs. It's no good, this whining and sniveling; if you can't go on living, then stick your head in an iron coal bucket to be bitten off."

That's right!

So Hamburg can be described.

Describing Dresden, though, is sure to be more work. But there is a solution—one to which our new Russian writers often resort.

Let's take some random detail of Dresden—for example, the fact that the automobiles there are ever so clean and upholstered on the inside with some gray, striped material.

The rest is simple—the way a crane lifts one ton.

One must categorize the whole of Dresden as gray-striped: the Elbe—a stripe against the gray; the houses—grayish; the Sistine Madonna—striped with gray. That will be far from true, of course, but very convincing and in the best of taste.

Gray-striped.

Berlin, on the other hand, is hard to describe—elusive, you might say.

In Berlin, as everyone knows, the Russians live around the zoo.

The notoriety of this fact is no cause for joy.

During the war, people said, "Everyone knows that the Germans usually launch an offensive in the spring"—as if Germans were an attribute of spring!

The Russians in Berlin promenade around the Gedächtniskirche the way flies circle around a chandelier. Fastened to the chandelier is a paper ball for catching flies; fastened to the *Kirche*, over the cross, is a strange, prickly nut.

The streets visible from the height of that nut are wide. The houses are as alike as suitcases. Ladies promenade in their sealskin coats and heavy, leather, high-button shoes; you, Alya, in your mouse-colored, seal-trimmed coat, walk among them.

Black marketeers promenade in their shaggy coats and so do Russian professors, two by two, clutching umbrellas behind their backs. There are many streetcars, but there's no point in riding around town, because one part of town is just like another. Palaces from some store that sells ready-made palaces. Monuments as alike as place settings. We are going nowhere: we huddle among the Germans like a lake between its shores.

There is no winter. The snow is either falling or melting.

Steeped in dampness and defeat, iron Germany is corroding and we, though not made of iron, are corroding along with her; we are being fused together by corrosion.

On Kleiststrasse, opposite the house where Ivan Puni lives, stands the house where Elena Ferrari lives.[2]

She has a porcelain face, with eyelashes so big that they drag down her lids.

She can slam them shut, like the doors of safes.

Between those two famous houses, the subway comes hurtling out of the earth; howling all the while, it mounts the platform of the elevated.

From the *Bahnhof* on Wittenbergplatz, which looks like a mole's burrow, the train runs, shrieking like a heavy shell on the rise, to the platform on Nollendorfplatz.

From there, the train slips behind a red *Kirche*. One *Kirche* in Berlin looks so much like another *Kirche* that we distinguish them only by the streets on which they stand.

The train slips behind the red *Kirche* through a breach in a house, as if passing through a triumphal arch.

Ahead lies the forum of all Berlin trains, Gleisdreieck. For the Russians, who live among the Germans as if between shores, Gleisdreieck is a transfer point.

From there, the train runs to Leipzigerplatz and to other squares, where beggars sell matches and seeing-eye dogs lie peacefully wrapped in their blankets.

The street-organs sob; they play neither *Ach, du lieber Augustin* nor *Deutschland, Deutschland über alles;* they simply moan. That sound is the mechanical moan of Berlin.

If you decide against riding to those squares, and walk instead through the deserted portals of the Gleisdreieck *Bahnhof*, you will see neither Germans, nor professors, nor black marketeers.

All around, along the roofs of the long yellow buildings, run tracks; tracks run along the ground and along high iron platforms, where they intersect other iron platforms as they rise to platforms still higher.

Thousands of fires, lanterns, spires, iron balls on three legs and semaphores—semaphores everywhere.

Despair, émigré love and streetcar no. 164 have brought me here; I have walked a long time on the bridges over the tracks that intersect here, just as the threads of a shawl drawn through a ring intersect.[3]

That ring is Berlin.

That ring for my thoughts is your name.

Often at night, in returning from your place, I passed under the twelve iron bridges.

I sang as I walked. I thought, why does life give only ready-made things to Gleisdreieck, the iron heart of Germany, and to the iron gates of Hamburg: houses like suitcases, streetcars that go nowhere. I walked along, returning home.

I took the road that passes under the twelve iron bridges.

I had far to go. Every night, on the corner of Potsdamerstrasse, I always saw the same prostitute in a red hat.

She hummed something when she saw me, then spoke in a language incomprehensible to me.

I kept walking; I had far to go.

What's to be done, comrade in the red hat!

There are many different animals on this earth and each of them praises and curses God in his own way.

You who have no words, you dive to the bottom of the sea and you bring from the bottom of the sea only sand as fluid as mud.

And I have many words and much strength, but she to whom I speak all my words is a foreigner.

~~~~Preface to Letter Nineteen

Alya's letter about aspirin, herring with potatoes, the telephone, the momentum of love, an English dancer and Stesha the wet nurse. The preface explains in detail why Alya's letter is not to be read.

Alya's letter is the best one in the whole book. But don't read it now. Skip it and read it after you've finished the book. I'll explain to you now why this must be done.

Even I didn't read it when it first arrived. I did kiss it and I skimmed certain passages, but it was written in pencil so I didn't read it.

Now I'll explain why. Listen carefully: her words fell on deaf ears. That is to say, I used to rivet boilers; I held the rivets from the inside by means of tongs. A thunderous noise in my ears. Now I see people's lips moving, but I hear nothing. Life has deafened me and deaf people are extremely remote.

I read Alya's letter only recently, on March 10, after I had already finished writing the book. I spent four hours reading it. First and foremost, the letter is very well written. Word of honor, I didn't write it. It contains the whole truth about the momentum of love and one other truth, unwritten, about the momentum of misfortune. I was bound to be broken while abroad and I found myself a love that would do the job. And without even looking at the woman, I immediately assumed that she didn't love me. I don't say that she would have loved me otherwise. But everything was predestined. This letter violates my format of two cultures, because the woman who wrote this about Stesha is one of us.

° And I love Stesha despite the fact that she rearranged all the furniture in me.°

Thus, dear friends, don't read this letter. To that end, I'm deliberately crossing it out with a red pencil. So that you don't read it by mistake.

What is the structural function of this letter? After all, it is included.

But, say—why the devil do you want structure? You insist? Then allow me! To make a work ironic, you need a double interpretation of the action, which is usually achieved by the technique of reduction—in *Evgenii Onegin*, for example, by the phrase "But is he not a parody?" In my book, though, I'm using the technique of enhancement to give a second interpretation of the woman I've been writing to; in addition, I'm providing a second interpretation of myself.

I am deaf.

If you believe my explanation of the structure, then you will also have to believe that the letter ascribed to Alya was written by me.

That would not be wise. . . .[1]

However, you will make neither head nor tail of all this. You see, the crucial sections were pruned by the proofreader.

Which is not to be read. It was written by Alya when she got sick. Though she used ruled stationery, this is the best letter in the whole book, but it is not to be read and has therefore been crossed out.

What can be written on this notebook paper? Just don't count the mistakes and don't give me any grades. I've chewed three aspirins, I've drunk an astonishing amount of various hot beverages, I've strolled barefoot around the apartment in my fur coat, I've talked to someone on the telephone, I've eaten herring with potatoes and I've done nothing for a long time, so now I'm writing you.

When I telephoned you, you came running to my place at a fast trot. What's that supposed to be? Conceit or just vileness—or both at the same time!

If you were a woman, my so-called Wertheim would be a tiny boutique next to your establishment.¹ But the momentum of your love frightens me a little. In fact, it's ghastly. You shout, you get irritated at the sound of your own voice, then you shout still more frantically. How, pray tell, will this momentum help you to declare your love to someone utterly unsuitable? Now don't lose your temper.

Get yourself a new suit and six shirts, so that three can be at the laundry and three at home; I'll give you a necktie; shine your boots.

And talk to me about books. I'll stand on my hind legs, be absolutely vertical and listen intently.

Now I'm going to sleep. I mustn't get sick or I won't be able to go dancing tomorrow.

Such a nice Englishman and dancer (two equally valuable assets). I mustn't get sick.

Such cold weather. I need either overshoes or a car. Should I pawn my soul to the devil? Maybe there's no harm if it's just in hock.

Yesterday I thought about my wet nurse Stesha all day long. There I was, thinking so hard that I took the wrong streetcar. Then I cried.

I'm more like Stesha than like Mama. Stesha is pink and white, plump, jolly, absolutely gentle and she loves the male sex. Which is why she was a wet nurse more than once.

She always came to see Papa on her way to the foundling home—no money.

Papa would scold her for not taking any from "that scoundrel."

"God be with him, master!"

She loved me like her own daughter. When I was two months old, she fed me cabbage soup and once she managed to poison me by gorging herself on the pits from the cherry preserves that were being made at our summer cottage. When I grew up, she came to see me, always with presents; she remained standing and spoke to me in the formal way; then, when everyone left, she sat down to drink tea with me and used the familiar form. When I became an adult, I began to understand her cheerful disposition: "My mistress lives with another woman; it's beyond me—just like nuns!" And she'd roar with laughter—such a completely warm woman. She had a special smell—like her wooden trunk when she lifted the lid: calico and apples. A tilted nose, knowing eyes.

The cook felt that too many young people were coming to see me and thought that all kinds of shocking things were going on behind the closed door. "Go on with you!" said Stesha; "they say you've had an illegitimate baby, but do you really think they've come to that?"

One time she was working in a very rich household. The house was robbed.

Stesha, as always, came to Papa in tears: they were going to haul her off to the police station.

Papa asked her: "And where were you when the house was robbed?"

"At the Novo-Devichy Convent visiting a nun."

"Well, then, tell them and they'll let you go."

"What? And get a nun mixed up in such a business, master!"

So she didn't say a word, but sat in prison until the thieves were found and she was released.

Then, after the revolution, Mama tried to persuade her to go vote, but she said that after that business with the silver spoons, she wouldn't go near the police station for love or money.

Long, long ago, she was promised a silk dress to wear at my wedding.

But she didn't get it. . . .

I love Stesha so much that I'm no longer sleepy.

I kiss you, my dear. If only I don't get sick!

Alya

Now what made me inflict Stesha on you?

Letter Twenty

Written at some time or other.

I lay at your feet like a rug, Alya!

Letter *Twenty-one*

The fifth one from Alya. In this letter she writes about the island of Tahiti, where everything is amiss. The schooners on the island smell of gasoline, which makes matters even worse. This island is too remote to be loved. It remains remote even when one lives there. The letter also tells about a horse named Tanyusha and about her voyage to the island of Moorea. The trip takes an hour and a half.

My Dear,

Tahiti is a place I love to remember, but hate to discuss. Mama always said that I have no sense when it comes to events and places. I have no idea about the number of inhabitants, black or white, on Tahiti or the length of its circumference in kilometers or the height of its mountains. Still, my thoughts return constantly to that dear island, that unbelievable sea. The water is as blue as ink; a coral reef encircles the island; the waves break against the reefs with a familiar sound and the foam forms a gigantic, white, imperishable garland. Behind the ear of each dark, smiling face is a tiara—a small, white flower, whose smell mingles constantly with the smell of vanilla. Crabs scuttle sideways along the shore; the sun sets behind Moorea. All this I know, see and feel.

However, that's beside the point. I wanted to tell you about Tanyusha. André gave me a dear little horse. In spite of the equator, the temperature and the coconuts, I called her Tanyusha. I was very pleased when old black Tapu called her: "Tanyusa." I took care of her myself; I cleaned, fed and watered her. And she in turn was well disposed toward me. She would come to the terrace for bananas and nicker softly. When Tanyusha had fattened up and become shiny and beautiful, her character suddenly changed: she didn't want to be mounted. Whenever I got on her, she began to balk and fidget, then to move backwards. It made no difference what was behind her—water, a prickly fence or people. And then she ran away for good—deep into the interior of the island—just try to find her! As luck would have it, André was gone. He was often away, visiting the other islands. And my bedroom had five doors and a window! All wide open! The nights on Tahiti are so soundless, so intense and so brilliant that even the blacks wouldn't set foot outside after dark. I was frightened to distraction—to tears. I finally thought of stationing Tapu in front of the door. Then, after Tanyusha ran away, I cried all night long. I cried often in those days. Tapu overheard and thought I was afraid that my husband would return and beat me because the horse had disappeared. The next morning, he said, "Do not cry. I will find Tanyusa and your *tane* (husband) will know nothing." He dispatched joyful black urchins in all directions and Tanyusha was restored.

When André returned and found out about her running away, he sold her at once. He dealt with horses as he did with people and considered that she had displayed ingratitude too base to tolerate. Tanyusha was loaded on a schooner and shipped to some Englishman on Moorea. How she must have been jostled, the poor thing!

You write about me—for yourself; I write about myself—for you.

Alya

Letter Twenty-three

An answer to the letter about Tahiti. It begins with reminiscences.
January is remembered, though the letter was written in the
middle of February. But the memories already seem
untrustworthy. The age of steam, electricity and the shimmy has
accelerated the tempo of life. The letter ends with an attempt
to write a dedication; the final paragraphs of the letter are offered
as an experiment in the pathetic style. So look at them in that
light.

(Second letter on the same day.)

You wrote about yourself for me.

You can smile for me, eat lunch for me or go anywhere
with anyone you please for me. I can do nothing for you.

You must have forgotten the words you wrote me on
a sheet of notebook paper.

If they were the truth, even for one minute, if you have
not forgotten them, then I too could write about myself for
you or at least about you for you.

But the notebook has been lost and these letters are not
grounds for an arraignment.

Forgive me, Alya, that the word "love" has again crept so
blatantly into my letter. I am tired of writing not about
love.

My letters are like our encounters: strangers are invariably present—a trio, a quartet and, more often than not, an entire chorus.

Set my words free, Alya, so that they can come to you °like dogs to their master and curl up at your feet.

Slippers size thirty-seven, gloves size six.°

Let me write about love.

But it's not worth crying about. Why, I'm as light-hearted and gay as a summer parasol.

Your letter is fine. Your voice is true—you don't falsetto. I'm even a trifle envious.

You've seen Tahiti, besides which writing comes easy to you.

You don't know—and that's just as well—that many words are forbidden.

Forbidden are words about flowers. Forbidden is spring. In general, all the good words are faint with exhaustion.

I'm sick of wit and irony.

Your letter made me envious.

How I want simply to describe objects as if literature had never existed; that way one could write literarily.

It would also be fine to write in long sentences something like: "Lovely is the Dnieper in quiet weather. . . ."[1] I too want to write about an "imperishable"—better yet, an "everlasting"—garland.

I will write about garlands, with an assist from your letter.

Alya, I can't hold back the words!

I love you. With rapture, with cymbals.

Those are words.

You have driven my love into the telephone receiver. That is said by me.

And the words say: "She is the only island for you in your

life. From her there is no turning back for you. Only around her does the sea have color."

And together we say:

Woman denying me access to yourself! Let my book curl up on your threshold like black Tapu. But it's white, my book. No, some other way. Without the reproach. Beloved! Let my book encircle your name, curl around it in a white, thick, unfading, imperishable, EVERLASTING GARLAND.

Letter Twenty-four

A cheerless letter, which does not distinguish it from the others. This one discusses the Germans, who know how to die, the women whom we are losing, Marc Chagall, the ability to hold a fork and the significance of provincialism in the history of art.[1]

You feel attached to the world of culture, Alya. To which one? There are many.

Every country has its own culture, which no foreigner can appropriate.

My heart aches for Petersburg: its streets are constantly on my mind. You, on the other hand, can't return to Russia because you love France, but you aren't likely to die of grief for her.

Your culture is all too pan-European.

If an automobile weighed nothing at all, it would not be able to go: its weight allows the wheels to grip.

I wouldn't have written you that if I didn't love you.

Don't torment me with the news that I weigh nothing as far as you're concerned; the world around Alya has no weight.

In the apartment next to Bogatyryov, a German family poisoned themselves with gas. The mother left a note: "There's no place in the world for the German worker."

Germans, I am ashamed that I can't help you! °You are

a great people—one that doesn't forget its native land. When you die, you die as Germans.°

Alya, forgive me my cheerless love: tell me, in what language will you speak your last words when you die?

I ply you with various charms; I hold you up to everyone. They say that a psychosis is like a monastery—a refuge. It's easier to imagine oneself as a dog than to live as a man.

I want to break into pieces and scatter throughout the city the fact that I love you.

If only I knew how!

One time several of us got together at a studio on Kleiststrasse. In the room were denizens of Petersburg and Moscow.

Someone broached the subject of visas. They say that, a year or two before, Russians had discussed passports with each other just as eagerly as married women talk about childbirth.

This time, too, the conversation somehow took that turn. The men, for the most part, had no passports at all and had come to terms with their new "life."

But the women!

There were French women, Swiss women, Albanian women (word of honor), Italian women, Czech women—chattering on and on, utterly absorbed.

It hurts men to lose their women.

I can well imagine what happened in Constantinople! ²

Such fates are terrible to behold. Our love, our marriages, our escapes—are nothing but motivations.

We are losing ourselves, becoming connective tissue.

Yet art needs the local, the vital, the differentiated (just the word for a letter!).

We will lose our talent as surely as we are losing our women.

You, Alya, are attached to culture; you know that you have good taste, but I love things of another taste. I love Marc Chagall.

I used to see Marc Chagall in Petersburg. It seemed to me that he resembled N. N. Evreinov; he was the spit and image of a small-town barber.[3]

Mother-of-pearl buttons on a gaudy vest. This man has ridiculously bad taste.

He transfers the colors of his suit and his small-town romanticism to paintings.

In his paintings, he is no European, but a Vitebskian.

Marc Chagall does not belong to the world of culture.

He was born in Vitebsk, a small, god-forsaken, provincial town.

Later, after the revolution, Vitebsk mushroomed; it acquired an important art school. Cities mushroomed with some frequency in those days: first Kiev, then Feodosia, then Tiflis . . . once even some village on the Volga—Markstadt —mushroomed with its very own academy of philosophy.[4]

So now every urchin in Vitebsk paints like Chagall and that is to his credit: he managed to remain a Vitebskian in Paris and St. Pete.

It's nice to know how to hold a fork, although that ability is shared by every hat-check girl in Europe. It's even better to know which shoes to wear with a smoking jacket and which cufflinks to stick into a silk shirt, though these accomplishments are of little use to me at the moment.

But I do keep in mind that in Europe everyone is European by birthright.

However, art needs its own smell and only a Frenchman smells French.

°A barbershop idea and nation [5] in art is no worse than any other.°

This is one area where thoughts about the salvation of the world are not too helpful.

It is useful, though, to introduce provincialism and cross it with traditional art. The balalaika players, "Carousel," the "Bluebird," etc., are bad in that they all counterfeit Russian provincialism.[6]

That gets people off the track. It hinders future work—paintings, novels.

Yet it's just as well that writing isn't easy—my friends always told me that.[7]

To live in any real way is painful.

In that respect, you are a big help to me, Alya.

Letter Twenty-five

About spring, the Prager Diele, Ehrenburg and pipes.[1] *About time, which passes, and lips, which renew themselves—about a certain heart that is being worn to a frazzle while the lips in question are merely losing their paint. About my heart.*

It's already forty-five degrees outside. My fall coat has become a spring coat. Winter is passing and, come what may, I won't be forced to endure a winter like this again.

Let's believe in our return home. Spring is coming, Alya. You told me once that spring makes you feel as if you've lost or forgotten something and you can't remember what.

When it was spring in Petersburg, I used to walk along the quays in a black cape. There the nights are white and the sun rises while the bridges are still drawn. I used to find many things on the quays. But you will find nothing; all you know is that something has been lost. The quays in Berlin are different. They're nice, too. It's nice to follow the canals to the workers' districts.

There, in some places, the canals widen into quiet harbors and cranes hover over the water. Like trees.

There, at the Hallesches Tor, out beyond the place where you live, stands the round tower of the gasworks, just like those at home on the Obvodny Canal. °When I was eighteen, I used to walk my girl friend to those towers every day.°

Very beautiful are the canals—even when the high platform of the elevated runs along their bank.

I am already beginning to remember what I've lost.

Thank God it's spring!

The little tables in the Prager Diele will be carried outdoors and Ilya Ehrenburg will see the sky.

Ilya Ehrenburg promenades in Berlin as he promenaded in Paris and in other cities full of émigrés—always bent over, as if looking on the ground for something he's lost.

However, that's an incorrect simile. His body is not bent at the waist: only his head is bent, his back curved. Gray coat, leather cap. Head quite young. He has three professions: 1) smoking a pipe, 2) being a skeptic, sitting in a cafe and publishing *Object*,[2] 3) writing *Julio Jurenito*.[3]

Later in time than *Julio Jurenito* is the book called *Trust D. E.*[4] Rays emanate from Ehrenburg; these rays bear various names; their distinctive feature is that they all smoke a pipe.

These rays fill the Prager Diele.

In one corner of the Prager Diele sits the master himself, demonstrating the art of smoking a pipe, of writing novels and of taking the world and his ice cream with a dose of skepticism.

Nature has endowed Ehrenburg lavishly—he has a passport.

He lives abroad with this passport. And thousands of visas.

I have no idea how good a writer Ilya Ehrenburg is.

His old stuff isn't any good.

But *Julio Jurenito* gives one pause. It is an extremely journalistic affair—a feuilleton with a plot, stylized character types and the old Ehrenburg himself, garnished with a prayer; the old poetry functions as a stylized character.

The novel develops along the lines of Voltaire's *Candide*—though with a less variegated plot.

Candide has a nice circular plot: while people look for Cunégonde, she is sleeping with everybody and aging. The hero winds up with an old woman, who reminisces about the tender skin of her Bulgarian captain.[5]

This plot—more accurately, this critical orientation on the idea that "time passes" and betrayals take place—was already being processed by Boccaccio. There the bethrothed woman passes from hand to hand and finally winds up with her husband, assuring him of her virginity.

The discoveries she made during her travels were not limited to hands. This novella ends with the famous phrase about how lips are not diminished but only renewed by kisses.[6]

But never mind, I will soon remember what I've forgotten. Ehrenburg has his own brand of irony; there is nothing Elizabethan about his short stories and novels. The good thing about him is that he chooses not to continue the traditions of "great" Russian Literature; he prefers to write "bad stuff."

I used to be angry with Ehrenburg because, in transforming himself from a Jewish Catholic or Slavophile into a European constructivist, he failed to forget the past. Saul failed to become Paul. He remains Paul, son of Saul, and he publishes *Animal Warmth*.

He is more, though, than just a journalist adept at organizing other people's ideas into a novel: he comes close to being an artist—one who feels the contradiction between the old humanistic culture and the new world now being built by the machine.

Of all these contradictions, the most painful to me is that while the lips in question are busy renewing themselves, the heart is being worn to a frazzle; and with it go the forgotten things, undetected.

Letter Twenty-six

About a mask, battery-powered engines, the length of the hood on the engine of the Hispano-Suiza; some general comments on internal-combustion engines and about how the Hispano-Suiza automobile would wear rings in its ears if it were a human being. Speaking as a driver, I'll say this: the letter is full of quiet fury and slander.

Today I woke up in the middle of the night. I was awakened by the incomprehensibility of the object in my hands.

The object proved to be a black paper mask and I found myself standing in the middle of the room.

It would clearly be a good idea for me to visit a sanatorium.

It's bad for me to talk about love.

Let's talk a bit about automobiles.

It's sad to ride in taxis!

The saddest thing of all, though, is to ride in a car with an electric engine. It has no heartbeat; it is filled with heavy batteries and they are charged, but the plates will lose their charge and the engine will stop. I've started a lot of cars in my day; sometimes they hit me with their cranks. I've helped a lot of people get started.

Sometimes, even in Berlin, I feel like starting an engine which some driver is unable to handle. I did that twice, but the third time I made a most humiliating mistake.

I walked up to start the engine and it was electric, with a false radiator and, of course, no crank. How do you start a car that has no heart, no crank to turn? It even looks artificial, like false shirtfronts and cuffs; the hood is put in front supposedly to cover an engine, but inside, more than likely, is nothing but rags.

They pretend to be internal-combustion engines.

Poor Russian emigration!

It has no heartbeat.

In Berlin, it is impossible and improper to speak Russian loudly on the streets. Why, the Germans themselves hardly speak above a whisper. Live, they say, but keep quiet.

Cruise around town, without noise and without hope, in a dead, battery-powered automobile. Run, without breathing, through whatever you once possessed; then, once you run down, die.

Our batteries were charged in Russia; here we keep going around in circles and soon we will grind to a halt. The lead battery plates will turn into nothing but sheer weight.

The acid will turn rancid.

The Russian newspapers in Berlin smell of this rancid weight.

Rancid and weighty are the words I have written.

We'd better talk about types of automobiles.

Do you like the Hispano-Suiza, Alya?

What a mistake! Don't give yourself away.

You love expensive things and you would gravitate to the most expensive things in any store even if all the price tags were scrambled the night before. The Hispano-Suiza? It's a bad car. An honest, noble car with a true stroke, a car with the driver sitting on one side to flaunt his impotence—that's the Mercedes, the Benz, the Fiat, the Delaunay-Belleville, the Packard, the Renault, the Delage and the very expensive but formidable Rolls-Royce, which has an unusually supple stroke. In all these cars, the design of the body follows the structure of the engine and the transmission; moreover, the design is calculated to minimize air resistance as much as possible. Racing cars usually have long noses, high in front: this particular shape, at high speed, offers the least resistance to the atmosphere. Have you ever noticed, Alya, that a bird flies with its blunt breast forward, not its pointed tail?

The length of an engine's hood is determined, of course, by the number of cylinders (four, six, occasionally eight or twelve) and by their diameter. The public is used to long-nosed cars. As for the Hispano-Suiza, it has a long stroke; that is, there's a great distance between the top and bottom centers of gravity. This car is extremely dubious and forced, so to speak—a cocaine sniffer if there ever was one. Its engine is high and narrow.

That's its own private affair.

But the hood is long.

Thus the Hispano-Suiza uses its hood as a disguise: there is a space of almost two feet between the radiator and the engine. That two feet is a lie made expressly for snobs; that two feet is a violation of good design and it infuriates me.

If I ever come to despise you, if I ever sing . . .

> Disappear, you paths
> On which I trod! [1]

. . . then I will consign my memory of you not to the devil, but to that void inside the Hispano-Suiza.

Your Hispano-Suiza is expensive, but worthless. Its chassis

often comes with folding seats instead of doors. That must appeal to gigolos.[2]

The steering wheel is set at an indecent angle; if the Hispano-Suiza were a man, it would have rings in its ears. Your Hispano-Suiza has its radiator in the wrong place. It runs around in false cuffs. It will never love you. All this I find more interesting than the life and times of the Russian emigration.

However, the Hispano-Suiza does hold the record for distance covered in mountainous terrain.[3]

Letter Twenty-seven

On the principle of relativity and the German with rings in his ears. Here too is included the folk tale about the little mouse that was turned into a girl.

Can a man make himself exotic by wearing rings in his ears?

Yes, but only at masquerades.

The man in question also wears foppish pants, but "too wide for a man with any self-respect"; in addition, he wears —in public—a beaver cap.

Yet you're head over heels in love with him!

What's to be done, Alya? You're teaching me the principle of relativity.

Nonetheless, here's a folk tale.

A hermit once fell in love with a mouse—a strange love, but in Berlin, loneliness will make a person do anything—and he turned her into a girl.

The girl did not love the hermit. He was jealous of her. She said to him: "So that's what your love is like!" She also said: "I want freedom, above all else. You'd better go away."

The hermit called her on the telephone and said: "Today is a nice day."

The girl said: "I'm not dressed yet."

The hermit said: "I'll wait. Let's go somewhere. I'll take you shopping."

The girl bought some things.

Then the hermit took her for a ride—to the Wannsee.

The sun was still visible.

Though no small number of stores had been visited.

He said: "Would you like to be the sun's wife?"

At that moment, a cloud covered the sun.

The girl said: "The cloud is mightier."

The hermit was compliant, especially with the girl.

He said, "Would you like the cloud for your husband?"

At that moment, the wind drove the cloud away.

The girl said: "The wind is mightier."

The hermit began to lose his temper.

The telephone had wrecked his nerves.

He shouted: "I'll get the wind for you."

The girl, irritated, retorted: "I don't need the wind. I'm warm and it's not blowing. I'm sheltered from the wind by that mountain. The mountain is mightier."

The hermit realized that women always take their time when they shop: the girl evidently thought she was at Marbach's. He answered patiently, like a clerk: "Then why don't you try the mountain!"

At that moment, the girl's face lit up. She became positively jubilant.

The hermit even imagined for a moment that he was happy.

She pointed one dainty finger at the foot of the mountain and said: "Look!"

The hermit didn't see anything.

"How handsome he is, how mighty! He's stronger than the mountain. There's a creature after my own heart! How well dressed he is!"

"Who, then?" inquired the hermit.

"That little mouse, dear hermit!" said the girl. "He's chewed his way through the mountain. Look, he loves me already."

"Splendid!" said the hermit; "if you really love him, go right ahead. It beats falling in love with someone who just stepped out of an operetta."

And he kissed the girl-mouse on her pink ears, set her free and presented her with a mouse passport. This type of passport, incidentally, is valid for any country.[1]

Letter Twenty-eight

Alya's last. In this one, Alya writes about how love letters should be written. The letter ends with the truculent sentence: "Quit writing about how, how, how much you love me, because at the third 'how much,' I start thinking about something else." The author of this book sincerely hopes that his readers never receive such letters.

You are violating our pact.

You are writing me two letters a day.

A lot of letters have accumulated.

I have filled the drawer of my writing desk; my pockets and my purse are overflowing.

You claim to know how Don Quixote is made, but you certainly don't know how to write a love letter.

And you're becoming more pesky all the time.

When you write about love, you choke on your own lyricism and froth at the mouth. . . . (I'm writing you from the "South" restaurant—sedate, alone, waiting for a schnitzel.)

I may not understand much about literature, though, being a flatterer, you assure me that I understand just as much as you. I do, however, know a lot about love letters. You're quite right to say that wherever I go, I know immediately what goes with what and who with whom.

You write about yourself, but when you write about me, you make reproaches. One doesn't write love letters for his own satisfaction, since no real lover thinks of himself when he's in love.

On various pretexts, you keep writing about the same thing. Quit writing about how, how, how much you love me, because at the third "how much," I start thinking about something else.

° *Alya* °

~~~~~~~~~~~~~~~Letter Twenty-nine

*The very last one. It is addressed to the All-Russian Central
Executive Committee. Once again, the twelve iron bridges are
mentioned. This letter contains a request for permission to return
to Russia. °At the end of the letter is placed a story about
Erzerum.°*

DECLARATION TO THE ALL-RUSSIAN
CENTRAL EXECUTIVE COMMITTEE

I cannot live in Berlin.

I am bound by my entire way of life, by all my habits, to
the Russia of today. I am able to work only for her.

It is not right that I should be living in Berlin.

The revolution transformed me; I cannot breathe without
it. Here one can only suffocate.

Bitter is the anguish of being in Berlin, as bitter as carbide
dust. Don't be surprised that this letter follows some letters
written to a woman.

I'm not getting a love affair involved in this matter. The
woman I was writing never existed. Perhaps there was
another, a good comrade and my friend, with whom I was
unable to come to terms. Alya is the realization of a
metaphor. I invented a woman and love in order to make a
a book about misunderstanding, about alien people, about
an alien land. I want to go back to Russia.

All that was has passed—my youth and self-assurance have been taken from me by the twelve iron bridges.

I raise my arm and surrender.

Let into Russia me and all my guileless luggage: six shirts (three at home, three at the laundry), a pair of tan boots accidentally polished with black wax, some old blue trousers in which I vainly attempted to make a crease.

°And a necktie which was given to me.

But the trousers I'm wearing have a crease. It was made when I was flattened into a pancake.

Don't let the history of Erzerum repeat itself. My friend Zdanevich happened to be riding down the road when that fortress was taken.[1]

On both sides of the road lay Turkish soldiers, hacked to death. In each case, the blows of the saber had fallen on the right arm and on the head.

My friend asked:

"Why were they all struck on the arm and head?"

He was told:

"Very simple. When Turks surrender, they always raise their right arm."°

~~~~~~~~~~Preface to the
Second Edition (1924)

So many words are forbidden.

As a matter of fact, all the good words are faint with exhaustion.

Forbidden are flowers, the moon, eyes and whole rows of words telling how pleasant it is to see.

Yet I would like to write as if literature had never existed— for example, "Lovely is the Dnieper in quiet weather."

I cannot; irony devours the words. It is needed, irony; it is the easiest way to overcome the difficulty of depicting things.

To depict the world as absurd is easiest of all.

And yet, at this moment, an enormous, almost authentic moon is peering into my window.

Among the trees, budding and bare, an automobile is disappearing into the long German road, into its depth.

These things are detached from each other. My house is far away.

Allow me to be sentimental. Life has hold of me in a foreign land and it does with me what it will.

I have no telephone to call Boris Eikhenbaum. Nor is

Tynyanov here. Roman no longer concerns himself with poetics.

I am alone.

A drunken soldier sobers up on his horse, but a lonely man is drunk beyond repair.

Except for Ivan Puni, I have no one in Berlin.

This is the plan of the book for you.

A man is writing letters to a woman.

She forbids him to write about love.

He reconciles himself to this and begins to tell her about Russian literature.

For him, this is a means of preening himself.

But then (behind the scenes) rivals appear.

Two of them: 1) an Englishman, 2) someone with rings in his ears.

The letters begin to turn yellow with rage.

A man who conducts himself in the Russian manner is as absurd in Europe as a fluffy dog in the tropics.

The woman materializes the mistake.

The mistake is realized.

The woman inflicts a blow.

The pain is real.

And the book is more serious than its preface.

But I am as garrulous in the introduction to my book as a woman who talks incessantly in order not to stop talking.

Preface to the
Third Edition (*1929*)

My °dear° past—you did exist.

The morning sidewalks of Berlin streets existed.

Marketplaces strewn with the white petals of flowering apple trees. Branches of the apple trees stood on the long market tables in pails.

Later, during the summer, there were roses on long branches; probably they were climbing roses.

Orchids stood in the flower shop on Unter den Linden and I never bought them.[1]

°I was in love—moving through the streets of Berlin as if under canvas. (Kind-hearted people will refrain from interpreting that last phrase literally.)

Then I revised this book when it was still painful to do so.°But for a long time now, what was cut from the heart has been borne away. I feel only pity for that past: the man that existed then.

°Now I have a hero, because the book is no longer written about me.° I left him (my former self) in this book as, in old-time novels, a sailor guilty of some offense was marooned on a desert island.

Live on, old friend, here it is warm and sentimental. Live on, old friend, I will not revise you.[2] Sit still and look at the sunset. The letters which were not in the first edition were actually written by you, but you did not send them then.

27 July 1928

P.S. I toss and turn with prefaces in this book like a man unable to sleep.[3]

First Preface to the Fourth Edition (1964)

A man is walking alone across the ice; fog is all around him. He believes that he is walking in a straight line. Wind disperses the fog: the man sees his goal, sees his tracks.

It turns out that the ice floe was floating and changing course: the trail is twisted into a knot—the man has gone astray.

I wanted to live and make decisions honestly: I did not want to shun what was difficult, but I lost my way. At fault and off course, I found myself an émigré in Berlin.

I have told that story in my book *A Sentimental Journey*, which has been published here at home twice; I am not republishing that one at the moment.

All this happened in 1922. I was miserable abroad. Within a year, owing to the efforts of Gorky and Mayakovsky, I succeeded in returning to my native land.

The book which you are about to read was written in Berlin; it is being published here for the third time.

Second Preface to the Fourth Edition (1964)

I am seventy years old. My soul lies before me.
It has been worn out by the bends in the road.
It was bent, at one time, by this book. I straightened it out.
The deaths of friends bent my soul. War. Quarrels. Mistakes. Insults. The cinema. And old age, which nonetheless came.
It is easier for me that I do not know the places where you walk, that I do not know your new friends or the old trees around your windmill.[1]
Memory has dispersed in widening circles. The circles have reached the stony shore. The past is no more.
The circles, rings of love, have receded, moving toward the shore.
I will not sit down beside the sea, I will not wait till kingdom come, I will not summon my fish with the golden freckles.[2]
I will not sit down at night beside the sea, I will not scoop water with an old, brown felt hat.
I will not say, "Sea, give me back the rings."

Night has already overtaken me. Stricken from the sky are the incomprehensible stars.

Only Venus, chief star of evening and morning, has returned to the sky. True to love, I love another.

In the morning, at an hour when one can see the shape of things quite clearly, I speak the word—Love.

The sun pours out into the sky.

The morning of song has no end: it is we who disappear.[3]

Let us view this book as water in whose passages the heart remained. So much of the past is contained in the blood and pride called lyricism.

1963. Moscow.

P.S. For several decades now, Alya has been a French writer, famous for her prose and the poems dedicated to her.

Which interrupts the continuity to make an important
announcement: things are altering man.

If I had owned an extra suit, I would never have come to
grief.

Just going home, changing clothes and pulling oneself
together alters an individual.

Women take advantage of this fact several times a day.

No matter what you say to a woman, demand an answer
immediately; otherwise, she'll take a hot bath, change her
dress and you'll have to say the whole thing all over again.

Changing clothes makes a woman forget even gestures.

I strongly advise you to demand a rapid answer from
women. Otherwise, you will find yourself constantly
bewildered by some new and unexpected statement.

A woman's life is almost devoid of syntax.

A man, however, is changed by his trade.

A tool not only extends the arm of a man, but also makes
him an extension of itself.

They say that a blind man localizes his sense of touch in
the end of his cane.

I feel no special attachment to my shoes, but they are, all
the same, an extension of me; they are part of me.

Then, too, the student was being changed by the trusty
cane, so it was prohibited.[1]

The monkey on his branch is more natural, but the branch still has an effect on his psychology.

And the psychology of the cow walking on slippery ice is proverbial.

What changes a man most of all is the machine.

In *War and Peace*, Lev Tolstoy relates how the shy and inconspicuous gunner Tushin finds himself, during battle, in a new world, created by his artillery:

Because of that terrible din, the noise, the necessity for concentration and activity, Tushin felt not the least unpleasant sensation of fear. On the contrary, he became more and more cheerful. . . . From the deafening sounds of his own guns around him, from the whistle and thud of the enemy's cannon balls, from the sight of the flushed, perspiring, hurrying gun crew, from the sight of the blood of men and horses, from the sight of puffs of smoke on the enemy's side (after which, each time, a ball flew past and struck the earth, a man, a gun or a horse)—from the sight of these things, there took shape in his mind a fantastic world, which was his sole pleasure at that moment. . . . He imagined himself an enormously tall, powerful man who was hurling cannon balls at the French with both hands.[2]

The machine gunner and the contrabassist are extensions of their instruments.

Subways, cranes and automobiles are the artificial limbs of mankind.

It so happened that I had occasion to spend several years among drivers.

Drivers change in proportion to the amount of power in the engines which propel them.

An engine of more than forty horsepower annihilates the old morality.

Speed puts distance between a driver and mankind.

Start the engine, press on the gas—and you have forthwith left space behind, while time seems measured only by the speedometer.

On a paved road, an automobile can do better than a hundred kilometers an hour.

But to what purpose is such speed?

It is needed only by a fugitive or his pursuer.

An engine attracts a man to what is accurately called crime.

Fortunately, the Russian driver is usually a good worker.

He drives on roads as choppy as waves and he repairs his car on the steppe, where the cold and gasoline freeze his hands.

But, at the same time, a driver is not a worker: he is alone in his car.

His car intoxicates him; speed intoxicates; speed divorces one from life.

Let's not forget the services of the automobile before the revolution.

It took some time for the Volhynian Regiment to make up its mind to leave the barracks.[3]

Russian regiments usually mutinied by standing in place.

The Decembrists were crushed where they stood.[4]

The Volhynians did leave their barracks, but they were hesitant. Coming to meet them were other groups.

The regiments were converging and coming to a halt.

But by then rocks were being thrown at the doors of the garages and workers in confiscated cars, with horns blaring, were streaming into the city.

You brought the revolution sloshing into the city like foam, O automobiles!

The revolution shifted gears and drove off.

The cars acquired bent springs and bent fenders; cars raced through the city and, wherever there were two, it seemed more like eight.

I love automobiles.

At that time, the whole country rocked and swayed. Then the revolution passed through its foamy period and left on foot for the front, °for the village.

But the cars went their own separate way, lived a life of their own.

Those who ran the country drove around in automobiles.

But those who ran only the cars also rode in them.

Sometimes by themselves.

Sometimes they looted—anything and anywhere. The booty was not enormous, but sometimes speed is its own reward.

Alcohol was being requisitioned by the government. Whenever some turned up, the drivers would rush to the spot with an order of their own devising and requisition it.

Sometimes they looked for a buyer and, as soon as he showed his money, that was requisitioned, too.

This was done by men whose minds were unable to cope with speed.

The alcohol sold by the drivers was a special kind, mixed with gasoline and creosote; cars ran on it.

Because Baku had been cut off.[5]

At that time, Russia had one kind of punishment—capital. Capital punishment was an everyday affair.

Revolvers were called "spalery."

That's dialect—in Yiddish, "spaler" means "spitter."

In one apartment where vodka was peddled, a sign on the wall said: "Alcohol may be consumed on the premises or taken out."

The owner wore a linen apron.

The death penalty was the norm for him; he viewed it the way a German views a fine.

Meanwhile, the country was crystallizing.

The gears were beginning to mesh.

The order and the pass made their appearance.

The most active speed demons were at the front.

And speed was justified there.

But in black Moscow—in Moscow, black and red, where the streets hardened as they wound around the Kremlin, just as dough winds around a paddle—in Moscow, people walked.

It was a city of pedestrians.

Then a gang made its appearance. Their big, black cars hugged the sidewalks—keeping quiet, keeping close to the curb.

They were particular.

When they found a woman to their taste, she was seized, dragged into the car and abducted with all the speed an automobile can muster at its most frenzied.

The women abducted were driven out of town and raped.

That went on in Moscow for several days.

During the inquest, one of the raped women had this to say about her experience:

"I was standing there shivering, with my fur coat draped over one arm.

"The driver asked: 'Why don't you put on your fur coat, miss?' "

(He called her "miss.")

"You'll just take it."

" 'We're not thieves.' "

But there were others with access to speed; they caught the gang.

When brought to trial, the gangsters confessed to everything. When asked, "Why did you do it?" they answered:

"We were bored."

They were killed.

I don't know their names and I'm not going to defend them.

But being a man with knowledge of speed and no sense of purpose, I would like to say a few words.

This isn't a graveside speech.

These men, fellow citizens, were no worse than any others.

They were just ordinary mechanics; they knew how to fix a car and they knew how cold iron can be when the temperature falls below freezing.

The speed of an engine and the blare of a horn knocked them off the track.

In Moscow, city of pedestrians, it was the engine that drove a driver to crime.°

A weapon makes a man bolder.

A horse turns him into a cavalryman.

Things make of a man whatever he makes from them.

Speed requires a goal.

Things are multiplying around us—there are ten or even a hundred times more of them now than there were two hundred years ago.

Mankind has them under control, but the individual man does not.

The individual needs to master the mystery of machines; a new romanticism is needed or machines will throw people out of life on the curves.

At the moment, I am bewildered, because this tire-polished asphalt, these neon signs and well-dressed women—all this is changing me.

Here I am not as I used to be; here, it seems, I fall short.

Letter Thirty-one

This letter constitutes an essential chapter in The History of the Russian Intelligentsia.[1] *It contains the word "teaser." The entire letter is indecent, so I'm hoping it wasn't sent.*[2]

You're right, Alya. I did make a fool of myself with that Englishman.

But I see myself at a remove; I fear my destiny.

I fear its literary quality. I am becoming part of a book.

Russian literature has a bad tradition.

Russian literature is devoted to the description of unsuccessful love affairs.

In the French novel, the hero is a success.

Our literature, from a man's point of view, is one continuous jeremiad.

Poor Onegin—Tatyana is consigned to another man.

Poor Pechorin without his Vera.

Lev Tolstoy, a writer who strikes no poses, decribes the same misfortune.

Who could possibly be more charming than Andrei Bolkonsky? [3]

Intelligent, brave, well bred, he talks like Tolstoy and is even disdainful of women.

But in a French novel, the hero would be not he, but Anatol Kuragin.

A fop and a swine.

He would get Natasha—and Maria, to boot.

Andrei Bolkonsky is in the same foolish predicament as all the heroes in *The History of the Russian Intelligentsia.*

Chaplin said that the most comical effects are obtained when a man in an unlikely situation pretends that nothing has happened.

It is comical, for instance, when a man hanging upside down attempts to straighten his tie.

We all go through life straightening our ties.

But my tie (the one you gave me, Alya) still chafes my neck.

And I, having gotten myself into a literary predicament, don't know what to do.

One is evidently expected to make humorous remarks and to express himself somewhat freely.

Very well.

When horses are breeding (it's positively indecent, but without it there wouldn't be any horses), the mare often gets nervous; some protective reflex sets in (I may not have it quite right) and she refuses to yield.

She may even kick the stallion.

The stud (Anatol Kuragin) is not destined for unsuccessful love affairs.

His path is strewn with roses; only utter exhaustion can terminate his romances.

Anyway, a pint-sized stallion is brought in—he may have a really beautiful soul—and led up to the mare.

They flirt with each other, but just as soon as they begin to work things out (in a manner of speaking), the poor little stallion is seized by the scruff of his neck and dragged away.

The pint-sized stallion is called a "teaser."

In Russian literature, he is required to utter several noble words after his exploit.

Being a teaser is no easy job; they say that sometimes it ends in insanity and suicide.

That particular job is the destiny of the Russian intelligentsia.

The hero of the Russian novel is a teaser.

I wanted to name a certain specific hero.

But I can't; he might take offense.

We played the role of teasers in the revolution.

That is the destiny of transitional groups.

The Russian emigration is an organization of political teasers who lack class awareness.

Otherwise, they wouldn't dare to show their faces.

What agony!

Even so, I'm not going to write about love.

You see, Alya? I never write about anything but literature.

Letter Thirty-two

About the Japanese Taratsuki and his love for Masha. About the lamentable resemblance between people of all colors. About Fujiyama. The letter ends with a reproach.

I'm very sentimental, Alya. That's because I take life seriously. Maybe the whole world is sentimental—that world whose address I know. It doesn't dance the foxtrot.

When I was in Russia in 1913, I had a student—a Japanese. His name was Taratsuki.

He worked as a secretary in the Japanese embassy.

And in the apartment building where he lived was a chambermaid named Masha, from the town of Soltsy. Everyone fell in love with Masha—caretakers, tenants, soldiers and the mailman.

She had everything she needed. She even had a little six-year-old girl back in Soltsy who called her mama "dummy."

It was warm in Taratsuki's room. I often sat beside him and read Tolstoy to him.

I always read too fast.

Taratsuki's face and my face would be reflected in the mirror on the wall.

My face changes constantly; his face was immobile, as if covered not with skin but with a shell.

It seemed to me that, of the two of us, probably only one was human.

For me, his world had no address.

Taratsuki fell in love with Masha. She would shriek with laughter when she talked about it.

He always accompanied her when she went walking with her little white dog.

Taratsuki loved her during 1914, 1915, 1916, 1917 and 1918.

Five years.

One time he went to see her and said:

"Listen, Masha. I have a grandmother. She lives in a garden on a big mountain called Fujiyama. She is very aristocratic and she loves me. That garden is also inhabited by her beloved white monkey."

(Don't be surprised at Taratsuki's style—after all, he learned his Russian from me.)

"Not long ago, the white monkey ran away from my grandmother.

"Grandmother wrote me about it.

"And I replied that I love a girl named Masha and requested permission to marry. I wanted you to be taken into the family.

"Grandmother replied that the monkey had returned, that she was very glad and that she consented to the marriage."

But Masha thought it hilarious that Taratsuki had a yellow grandmother on Fujiyama.

She just laughed and kept wanting nothing.

Then came the revolution.

Taratsuki hunted up Masha, who was out of work, and once again pleaded with her:

"Masha, no one understands anything here. This will not be over soon. There will be a lot of blood.

"Let us go to my home in Japan."

The revolution continued.

Taratsuki asked Masha to come to the embassy. Everything at the embassy was being packed. Masha went.

There they were received by the ambassador, who hurriedly said:

"Young lady, you do not realize what you are doing. Your fiancé is a wealthy and aristocratic man. His grandmother has given her consent. Stop and think. Do not let happiness pass you by."

Masha said nothing.

But when they went outside, Masha replied to her Japanese: "I'm not going anywhere," whereupon she planted a kiss on his shaved head.

Taratsuki presented himself before her one more time. He was very sad. He said:

"Dear Masha. If you will not go, then give me the little white dog with which you go walking."

Since there was a famine and nothing to feed the dog, Masha gave her to the Japanese.

The last letter from Taratsuki came from Vladivostok.

This is what the letter said:

"I have brought your dog to this place and will soon be going on with her. It will be very difficult for you in your country. I await an answer. Write and I will come for you."

But hardly had the letter arrived when the railroad was blown up in hundreds of places.

But Masha would not have answered, anyway. She remained.

As before, she was loved by everyone. She was not afraid of the revolution, because she had no aristocratic yellow grandmother.

Now she works in a plant called "Military Medical Products"—something like that.

Whenever she remembers the Japanese, she feels sorry for him.

Everyone loves her. She's a real woman. She seems as nameless and selfless as a blade of grass. She lives without taking notice of herself.

I too feel sorry for the Japanese.

And I think about how wrong I was to look in the mirror and conclude that the Japanese and I were different.

He's a lot like me, that Japanese.

That fact, I suspect, is not likely to facilitate the expansion of his country's military might.

But you, Alya, are not Masha.

Your sky contains no stars—just your address. All this, however, is less than ideal—much less.

—————————Letter Thirty-three

A short one.

    Even though you write your blue letters to other people, I love you.[1]

Alya

Letter Thirty-four

With a complaint to the effect that sorrow is too brief. He is
too exacting for someone of so little staying power. He is
sorrowful enough to warrant a handkerchief. In addition,
this letter provides a variant of a famous fairy tale.[1]

So help me, Alya . . . I'll be finishing my novel soon.

O woman refusing to answer me!

You have driven my love into the telephone receiver.

My sorrow comes to see me and sits at the same table with me.

I have conversations with him.

Yet the doctor says that my blood pressure is normal and that my hallucination is only a literary phenomenon.

Sorrow comes to see me. I talk to him while inwardly counting up pages.

There are only a hundred pages or so.

Such a brief sorrow!

I should have gotten a different brand—one international in scope.

Then everything might have happened differently.

But it proved impossible.

All I could do was to get six shirts, as you instructed.

"Three at home, three at the laundry."

I was bound to be broken and I found myself a love that would do the job.

A man was sharpening a knife against a stone. The stone was not important to him, though he bent over it.

That's from Tolstoy.

His version of it is longer and better written.[2]

My fate was completely predetermined.

But everything might have been different.

Suppose I provide the romance with an alternative denouement.

Taken from Andersen.[3]

This is what might have happened.

Once there was a prince.

He had two treasures: the rose growing on his mother's grave and a nightingale which sang so sweetly that a man could become oblivious of his own soul.

He fell in love with a princess from the neighboring kingdom and sent her:

1) The rose.

2) The nightingale.

The princess gave the rose to an instructor at the skating rink and the nightingale died on her three days later: it couldn't stand the smell of eau de cologne and powder.

As for the rest of the story, Andersen has it all wrong.

On no account did the prince disguise himself as a swineherd.

Instead, he borrowed money to buy silk stockings and slippers with pointed toes.

It took him one day to learn to smile, two days to learn to keep quiet and three months to get used to the smell of powder.

He gave the princess:

1) A rattle to dance the shimmy to.

2) A special toy that gossiped—probably some book with a dedication.

The princess really did kiss him.

And the night on which the princess came to the prince really was black and rainy.

The princess knocked boldly.

The prince slid down the banister: he thought he heard knocking every night of the week, so he had thoroughly mastered the art of sliding down banisters.

He opened the door and (let's try some cubism) the wind hurled into the rectangle prisms of rain and the spherical sectors of an umbrella.

The prince recognized the umbrella instantly.

He bowed down even lower than his feet (he was standing on the threshold) and he said:

"Enter my humble abode, princess."

She entered. After all, it was raining.

She was so exhausted that she went upstairs without even closing the umbrella.

The prince sat her down in front of the fireplace, lit the fire, set the table and ran immediately to fetch:

1) The rose.

2) The nightingale.

The prince tended to be absent-minded.

It was then that the fried fish began to laugh.

Fried fish always laugh in oriental fairy tales. I'll go into the details in my other books.

As far as I know, this is the first time a fried fish has laughed in European literature.

It laughed to see someone giving his heart instead of a rattle.

This time it laughed itself sick, flopped its tail and splashed the sauce.

"Prince," it said, "why spoil foreign fairy tales?"

"Andersen has slandered me," replied the prince.

"My house and my heart belong to the princess.

"The loved one is never to blame.

"And you lie still and quit splashing the sauce, because the princess is going to eat you now."

"You're well chewed yourself, O half-baked prince," said the fish.

Having thus spoken, it died a second time—this time, of boredom: it didn't love the princess.

And here's another possible denouement for the romance.

The princess lives in the same house as the prince, because there are very few vacant apartments in the city.

The prince becomes a toysmith: he fixes phonographs and makes rattles to dance the shimmy to.

The princess eats and sleeps in his house.

But she sleeps with others.

It turns out that between a given point and a straight line, one can draw several perpendiculars.

All this makes sense if one knows non-Euclidean geometry well or if one reaches the point where a pun amuses him about as much as an ulcer.

It's all a question of "how much."

All my letters are about "how much" I love you.

Postscript

Germany.

A crushed Germany. Three hundred thousand Russians in Berlin.

Russian restaurants, where naval officers wait on tables.

In one such restaurant sits a former general, ordering borsch for some former officers. He speaks in German.

They speak in Russian—to refresh his memory. That's all right—through them, the service will improve.

Outside the confines of Russia, we became a nation of Rumanians and gypsies. Russian culture refused to emigrate, so we left it behind. Lots of books in Germany sell better than Krasnov's *Beyond the Thistle*.[1]

And no one has any use for theory of poetry.

We were plucked from Russia like a sieve from the water.

Dark and incomprehensible is the smoke of northern, working-class Berlin.

Smoke hovers over the gray water of Hamburg.

Incomprehensible Germany quivers.

The only comprehensible thing in Berlin is Westen. Here the streets are wide, the asphalt rubbed smooth by automobile tires. Westen is comprehensible and so is that fact that soon it will be no more.

And how hard it is to look at a German! At a teacher, doctor, intellectual, clerk.

They are beginning their dark, tortuous journey between west and north.

Beginning it with revolution and with those opposed to revolution.[2]

The old Germany has disintegrated.

The fragments of the old army haunt cafés and indulge in pederasty.

The streets are filled with terribly subdued cripples.

Three hundred thousand Russians of various nationalities wander aimlessly in the cracks of a perishing city.

The cafés are filled with music.

An enclave of waiters and singers within a conquered nation.

Meanwhile, in the dark public toilets of Berlin, men indulge in mutual onanism. They are suffering from a devalued currency and hunger; their country is perishing.

And slowly, gobbling up the spoils, foreigners pass among them.[3]

The whole thing is simple—straightforward and elementary.

Down with imperialism.

Long live the brotherhood of peoples.

If one must perish, let it be for that.

Was it conceivably for this piece of knowledge that I journeyed so far?

Transliteration System

For Russian words and titles, this work follows the Library of Congress system of transliteration, with diacritical marks omitted. For proper names—with the exception of such names as Tolstoy, Ehrenburg, and Moscow, already familiar in another spelling—the following system has been used.

а a		п p	
б b		р r	
в v		с s	
г g		т t	
д d		у u	
е e		ф f	
ё yo (o *after* sh, zh, *and* ch)		х kh	
ж zh		ц ts	
з z		ч ch	
и i		ш sh (s *before* t)	
й i		щ shch	
ый y		ъ (*omitted*)	
ий y		ы y	
к k		ь (*omitted except* i *before* e)	
л l		э e	
м m		ю yu (u *in the word Lusya*)	
н n		я ya (a *after* i)	
о o			

Author's Preface

°The material between the circles was omitted from a later edition, in this case the fourth edition—a circumstance which will henceforth be indicated in the following way: °4e. Insignificant changes—those involving only a word or two—will usually not be indicated. The omission of an entire letter in later editions is noted below.

1. *Zavetnye skazki*, a collection of erotic folk tales compiled by A. N. Afanasev (1826–1871). (An English translation, called *Russian Secret Tales*, was published by Brussel and Brussel, Inc., in 1966.) In his book *O teorii prozy* [Theory of Prose] (Moscow and Leningrad, 1925), Shklovsky frequently uses them to illustrate his theory of estrangement—the technique of depicting things from a new and striking point of view. In the given case, he means, for example, the tendency in these tales to speak of the sexual organs in metaphoric fashion: lock and key, mortar and pestle, bow and arrow, etc.

Menagerie

1. A vantage point in the Central Urals which Khlebnikov visited in 1905 as member of an ornithological expedition.

2. Russia's medieval masterpiece was reputedly discovered in a collection of manuscripts belonging to a monastery. Medieval monks frequently copied literary works into their chronicles. Like a Book of Hours, *The Lay of Igor's Host* is adorned with animals of marvelous potentialities.

3. *Sadok sudei* (Petersburg, 1909), which may mean either a trap or a hatchery for judges. This was the first document issued by the Russian futurists. It actually appeared in April 1910 in an edition of three hundred copies, which were printed on wallpaper as a parody of elaborate "bourgeois" books. Khlebnikov's poem, one of the few outstanding works in this collection, shows the influence of Walt Whitman, whose poems had been translated by Kornei Chukovsky in 1907. See Vladimir Markov, *Russian Futurism: A History* (Berkeley and Los Angeles, 1968), chap. i.

Letter One

This letter was omitted from 2e.

1. In 4e, the date was changed to 3 February, which eliminates the chronological disorder of the first three letters.

Letter Two

This letter was omitted from 2e.

Letter Three

This letter was omitted from 2e.

Letter Four

1. Viktor (Velimir) Vladimirovich Khlebnikov (1885–1922), influential poet who helped found the futurist movement in Russia.

2. Yuly Isaevich Aikhenvald (1872–1928), a popular prerevolutionary critic, known especially for his work *Silhouettes of Russian Writers,* 1906. Along with dozens of other dissident intellectuals, he was expelled from Russia in the fall of 1922, at which time he became Shklovsky's neighbor. His approach to literature, mystical and impressionistic, stressed the sacerdotal role of the writer—a conception of criticism anathema to Shklovsky.

3. *Vzial: Baraban Futuristov* [Took: Drum of the Futurists] (Petrograd, 1915), an almanac containing articles and poems by the futurists, including Shklovsky and Mayakovsky. Khlebnikov described his utopia in the article entitled "Predlozheniia" [Proposals].

4. In 3e, the following footnote was added: "The name of this creature is Gornfeld." In 4e, the note simply says: "Gornfeld." This is Arkady Georgievich Gornfeld (1867–1941), a critic interested primarily in the nature of the creative process—an approach scorned by Shklovsky.

5. Pyotr Vasilevich Miturich (1887–1956), an artist who befriended Khlebnikov during the last year of his life and who married Khlebnikov's sister. As early as 1914, Khlebnikov attempted to found an international society that would be a sort of world government. At first called the Society of 317, it eventually acquired the name Society of Presidents of the Globe. See Vladimir Markov, *The Longer Poems of Velimir Khlebnikov* (Berkeley and Los Angeles, 1962), chap. ii, from

which the information about Khlebnikov in these notes has been taken.

6. During 1919 and 1920, Khlebnikov lived in Kharkov, where he was, at various times, arrested by both the Reds and the Whites. During this period, he joined forces with the imagists, a peripheral group of poets who delighted especially in the juxtaposition of dissonant images.

°4e.

7. A prerevolutionary artists' colony located not far from the Gulf of Finland. Now part of Russia, it is called Repino after one of its most famous inhabitants, the painter Ilya Efimovich Repin (1844–1930).

8. Written by Khlebnikov in 1909 and published in the notorious futurist almanac *Poshchechina po obshchestvennomu vkusu* [A Slap at Public Taste] (Moscow, 1912).

9. Nikolai Ivanovich Kulbin (1868–1917), an eccentric doctor who actively promoted the new trends in Russian art among the inhabitants of Petersburg. He wrote articles, sponsored exhibitions, and subsidized impoverished young people of talent (including Shklovsky). For Ivan Puni, see Letter 15.

10. In 3e and 4e, this sentence has been expanded to read: "The waves were like corrugated, galvanized iron—the kind used for washing clothes."

11. Vasilisa Georgievna Kordi, Shklovsky's first wife.

°2e, 3e, 4e.

Letter Five

1. Aleksei Mikhailovich Remizov (1877–1957), a brilliant and influential writer who attempted in his prose to strip the Russian literary language of its foreign derivations and restore to it the natural raciness of the vernacular. He emigrated from Russia at

the end of 1921 and settled in Berlin until 1923, when he moved
to Paris, where he remained until his death. Remizov founded
his monkey society as a lampoon on the official organizations
and committees that proliferated after the revolution. Charter
memberships were conferred by elegantly designed scrolls,
signed by Asyka, tsar of the monkeys.

2. Aleksandr Aleksandrovich Blok (1880–1921), greatest of
the symbolist poets; Mikhail Alekseevich Kuzmin (1875–1936),
symbolist poet and author of ballets, operettas, and plays; for
Grzhebin, see Letter 7.

3. In the spring of 1919, Shklovsky traveled from Petrograd
to Kherson to get his wife. They were trapped there when
General Wrangel launched an offensive that summer. Shklovsky
joined the Red Army, which soon repelled Wrangel's Whites.

4. A reference to Rudyard Kipling's story "The Cat That
Walked by Himself" (1902), one of the *Just So Stories*. It
relates how man and his wife tamed the animals by luring them
to their cave with food and comfort. The cat refused to be
bribed and finally won certain privileges on its own terms from
the woman.

5. In 4e, the "Our" becomes "Their."

6. *Rossiia v pis'menakh* (Berlin, 1922); the book based on
Rozanov's letters is *Kukkha: Rozanovy pis'ma* [Kukkha:
Rozanov's Letters] (Berlin, 1923). Vasily Vasilevich Rozanov
(1856–1919), a close friend of Remizov, also played a seminal
role in the development of Russian prose. His attempt to
approximate the informality of conversation in his writing
exerted a strong influence on Shklovsky. "Kukkha" is a word
defined by Remizov as meaning "moisture" in monkey language.
°4e.

7. For Bely, see Letter 9. "Syntheses" probably refers to
Gorky's unrealized dream of achieving a *rapprochement* between
Soviet Russia and the emigration through his journal *Colloquy*,

also intended as a vehicle for transmitting Western ideas to Russia. Eugen Steinach (1861–1944) was an Austrian physiologist commissioned by Gorky to write an article for *Colloquy* on his experiments in rejuvenation, which he attempted to achieve by transplantations of the sex glands and injections of sex hormones.

8. Solomon Gitmanovich Kaplun (Sumsky) (1891–1940), a Menshevik who lived in Berlin from 1922 to 1925. He owned the Epoch Publishing House, which published Gorky's journal *Colloquy*. Maria Fyodorovna Andreeva (1872–1953) was Gorky's common-law wife. Kaplun appeared in Remizov's story "Pered shapochnym uborom" [Before the Final Curtain]; Andreeva appeared in the lament for Blok, entitled "K zvezdam" [To the Stars]. The journal which originally published these stories has not been ascertained, but they were reprinted in Remizov's book *Vzvikhrennaia Rus'* [Russia in Vortex] (Paris, 1927).

Shklovsky subscribed to the futurist notion that form dictates content; consequently, Kaplun and Andreeva appear in these pieces as a result of Remizov's choice of an open form, hospitable to details not usually considered eligible for "literature."

°Moving . . . . 2e.

°We play . . . . 3e, 4e. In 2e only, this sentence remains and is followed by the sentence: "And I'm content—I'm an artist, as cheerful and light-hearted as a bright summer parasol."

9. "Rozy" and "morozy," a hackneyed rhyme mocked by Pushkin in *Evgenii Onegin*, chap. iv, stanza 42.

Letter Six

1. In 2e, 3e, and 4e, a postscript has been added: "P.S. The ape died."

Letter Seven

This letter was omitted from 3e and 4e.

1. Zinovy Isaevich Grzhebin (1869–1929), an artist who became editor of the journals *Parus* [Sail] and *Shipovnik* [Sweetbriar] and then owner of a publishing house connected with Gorky's project to publish all the classics of world literature in Russian translation. Grzhebin emigrated at the end of 1920, spent a few months in Stockholm, then settled in Berlin, where he founded the most important émigré publishing house.

2. Yury Pavlovich Annenkov (b. 1889), artist, director, and writer. A color reproduction of the portrait may be found in Annenkov's book *Portrety* (Petrograd, 1922), p. 67.

3. This couplet may be a paraphrase of the first three lines in Pushkin's poem "Domik v Kolomne" [The Cottage in Kolomna].

Letter Eight

This letter was omitted from 2e.

Letter Nine

1. Shklovsky wrote an important article entitled "Kak sdelan 'Don-Kixot'" [How Don Quixote Is Made], which was published in the journal *Zhizn' iskusstva* [The Life of Art], 1921; reprinted in his book *Razvertyvanie siuzheta* [Plot Progression], 1921, and in *Theory of Prose*, 1925.
  °2e.

2. Andrei Bely (Boris Nikolaevich Bugaev, 1880–1934),

symbolist poet whose novels influenced Russian prose during the early twenties, and whose criticism laid the foundation for the work of the Russian formalists. Disturbed by the death of Blok and the execution of Gumilyov in August 1921, Bely applied for an exit visa; the Bolshevik regime, eager to counter the bad impression left by those deaths, gave him one. He settled in Berlin in the fall of 1921 and remained there until October 1923. At that time, he was on the verge of settling in Prague, with the encouragement of Marina Tsvetaeva, but he abruptly changed his mind and returned to Russia. See Oleg Maslenikov, *The Frenzied Poets: Andrey Biely and the Russian Symbolists* (Berkeley, 1952).

3. In 4e, this sentence has been expanded to read: "His eyes are cut in an angular fashion." Nearly everyone writing about Bely has commented on his singularly compelling eyes.

4. Bely wrote, all together, four "Symphonies" between 1902 and 1908. The reference is probably to the first one, entitled *Simfoniia* (*vtoraia, dramaticheskaia*) [Symphony (Second, Dramatic)].

5. A philosophical movement founded by Rudolph Steiner (1861–1925), an Austrian social philosopher. Bely lived in the anthroposophical colony at Dornach, Switzerland, between 1914 and 1916 and always retained his interest in the philosophy, which purported to reconcile the differences between science and mysticism. Anthroposophy postulated ideal spiritual worlds accessible only to those who divested themselves of their materialistic orientation, and who developed powers of cognition independent of the senses and the intellect.

6. *Zapiski chudaka* [Notes of an Eccentric] (Berlin, 1922). "Stepped" (*stupenchatyi*) is a critical term coined by Shklovsky to designate works of literature which unfold in a linear fashion. *Kotik Letaev* (Berlin, 1922) is considered by D. S. Mirsky as Bely's most original work. It deals with the

infancy of Kotik, from his prenatal impressions to his gradual cognition of the external world.
°2e.

Letter Ten

This letter was omitted from 2e.

1. *Obshchestvo po izucheniiu poeticheskogo iazyka* [Society for the Study of Poetic Language], the coalition of linguists and futurists founded by Shklovsky in 1914 to study literature from the standpoint of style and structure; it grew into the full-fledged critical movement known as Russian formalism. In Russian, the pun is "opoiasan Opoiazom."
°4e.

2. This is a play on the Russian expression: "lit' vodu v chuzhuiu mel'nitsu"—literally, to pour water into the wrong mill, i.e., to play into someone's hands.

Letter Eleven

1. Pyotr Grigorevich Bogatyryov (b. 1893) returned to Czechoslovakia after his sojourn in Berlin and remained there—apparently on a mission for the Soviet government—until 1940, at which time he returned to the Soviet Union, where he became a specialist in Slavic folklore. The banknote in question was of a series issued by the Provisional Government of Aleksandr Fyodorovich Kerensky in 1917.

2. Ivan Ivanovich Grekov (1867–1934), eminent professor of medicine, whose wife presided over one of the most elegant salons in postrevolutionary Petrograd. Mikhail Leonidovich

Slonimsky (b. 1897), member of the Serapion Brothers and novelist.

3. In 3e and 4e, the following line has been added: "No one can make us ridiculous, because we work."

°4e.

4. Roman Osipovich Jakobson (b. 1896), a leading member of the Moscow Linguistic Circle. Jakobson emigrated to Prague in 1920, an act which Shklovsky strongly criticized in an open letter published in *Knizhnyi ugol* [The Book Niche], VIII (1922), where he accused Jakobson of having abandoned his work on poetics and urged him to return to Russia. Jackobson responded in his book *O cheshskom stikhe, preimushchestvenno v sopostavlenii s russkim* [On Czech Verse, as Compared Primarily to Its Russian Counterpart] (Berlin, 1923), which has the terse dedication: "To Viktor Shklovsky, in lieu of an answer to his letter in *The Book Niche*." Shklovsky's own emigration may have made him temporarily more sympathetic to Jakobson's position, but after he returned to Russia, he resumed his attacks in another open letter, part of his autobiography *Tret'ia fabrika* [The Third Factory] Moscow, 1926). The quarrel later intensified as a result of their differing interpretations of Mayakovsky's work.

°He takes . . . . 2e.

°Bogatyryov . . . . 4e.

5. *Cheshskii kukol'nyi teatr i russkii narodnyi teatr* (Berlin, 1922).

6. A Berlin restaurant frequented by Russians.

Letter Twelve

1. The Serapion Brothers, a group of young people who organized in February 1921 to learn how to write under the

collective aegis of Gorky, Shklovsky, and Evgeny Zamyatin. Their brilliant prose and poetry contributed in a decisive way to the regeneration of Russian literature after the revolution.

2. Aleksandr Ivanovich Kuprin (1870–1938), a short-story writer who began his career as a member of Gorky's Znanie (Knowledge) group, and who specialized in sensational stories braced with strong plots. Kuprin was living in Gatchina when it was occupied by the White army of General Yudenich in the fall of 1919. When the Whites withdrew in October, he accompanied them. After spending a few months in Finland, he moved to Paris, where he resided until his return to the Soviet Union in 1937.

3. Part VI, chap. ii.

4. Judges 7:4–8, where Gideon, gathering an army to lead against the Midianites, reduced his forces from 32,000 to a more workable 300 by the criterion discussed in the letter.

5. A reference to the Trojan émigré Aeneas, who, according to legend, gathered the survivors of ruined Troy and led them, after many adventures, to Italy, where they founded Rome.

6. Judges 12:1–6, where the Gileadite clan, led by Jephthah, defeated the Ephraimite clan. "Shibboleth" means "corn."

7. "Kukuruza" means "corn."

Letter Thirteen

1. Lines from a famous poem by Apollon Aleksandrovich Grigoriev (1822–1864).

°2e.

2. Benedikt Konstantinovich Livshits (1887–1939), poet and charter member of the futurist movement.

3. It was actually 1911.

°We slept . . . . 3e, 4e.

°When we . . . . 3e, 4e.
4. The Bogomils were a Bulgarian sect that flourished between 1000 and 1400 A.D. Its adherents believed that both Christ and Satan were sons of God and that it was Satan who created the visible world; hence, they denied the doctrine of incarnation and rejected the Christian conception of matter as a vehicle of grace. They rejected the whole organization of the Orthodox Church and its sacraments and avoided all contact with matter and flesh.
°2e.

Letter Fourteen

°2e.
1. An institution opened by Gorky in December 1919 as a meeting place and dormitory for promising young writers and artists. Shklovsky was living there before he fled to Finland, and it was the birthplace of the Serapion Brothers.

Letter Fifteen

1. Ivan Albertovich Puni (Jean Pougny, 1894–1956). He eventually settled in Paris, where he achieved success as a member of the Paris School of painting.
2. This exhibition, held in Petrograd in February 1915, was called the first futurist exhibition. It was underwritten by Puni and featured the works of Kazimir Malevich (1878–1935) and Vladimir Tatlin (1885–1953).
3. Carl Einstein (1885–1940), a German writer who produced experimental novels, poems, and plays.
4. *Gesellschaft mit beschränkter Haftung* [company with

limited liability]. In 4e, the equivalent Russian words are substituted for the German initials.

°4e.

Letter Sixteen

This letter was omitted from 2e.

Letter Seventeen

1. Boris Leonidovich Pasternak (1890–1960), outstanding poet and author of *Dr. Zhivago*. Pasternak visited Berlin early in 1923 to see his parents and two sisters, who had emigrated in 1921.

°2e.

2. Part II, chap. ii. In this scene, Tolstoy uses counterpoint to heighten the contrast between the disagreeable young officers and the marching soldiers. The unpleasant exchange between Dolokhov and his comrade is periodically interrupted by snatches of the song sung by the troops.

3. Marina Ivanovna Tsvetaeva (Efron) (1892–1941), highly original poet who returned to the Soviet Union in 1939 and committed suicide two years later. She made this comment in her ecstatic review of Pasternak's collection of verse *Sestra moia zhizn'* [Sister Mine—Life] (Berlin, 1922). Her review, entitled "Svetovoi liven'" [A Luminous Shower], appeared in *Epopeia* II (1922) and was reprinted in the American collection of her prose entitled *Proza* (New York, 1953).

°important . . . . 4e.

°A happy . . . . 4e. These omissions, of course, reflect the scandal that surrounded the publication of *Dr. Zhivago* abroad in 1957 and the award of the Nobel Prize to Pasternak in 1958. The treatment accorded Pasternak at that time made it clear that Shklovsky's prediction had been unduly optimistic.

4. Pasternak spent the summer of 1912 studying philosophy at the University of Marburg. Late in 1922, he married Evgenia Vladimirovna Lure, a painter previously married to the minor novelist and critic Pavel Pavlovich Muratov (1881–1950), who emigrated to Berlin during the early twenties. In 1930, Pasternak divorced his wife to marry Zinaida Nikolaevna Eremeeva, wife of Genrikh Gustavovich Neigaus (b. 1888), noted pianist and authority on Chopin. Neigaus, after divorcing his wife, married Evgenia Vladimirovna.

Ilya Ehrenburg, in his memoirs, mentions *Zoo* and confirms that Pasternak was indeed happy during this period. But Ehrenburg takes issue with Shklovsky on the question of propulsion, saying that Pasternak was sensitive to many things and many people, but never to history. See Ilya Ehrenburg, *People and Life, 1891–1921* (New York, 1962), pp. 280–281.

°4e.

Letter Eighteen

1. A Belgian make of revolver adopted by the Russian army at the end of the nineteenth century.

2. Elena Konstantinovna Ferrari (Olga Fyodorovna Golubeva, 1899–1939), an aspiring poet who complained in a letter to Gorky dated October 6, 1922, that Shklovsky was terrorizing her with his advice on her writing. See *Gor'kii i sovetskie pisateli* [Gorky and Soviet Writers], Vol. LXX of *Literaturnoe nasledstvo* [Literary Heritage] (Moscow, 1963), p. 567.

3. The linen shawls made at Orenburg were so fine that they could be drawn through a ring.

Preface to Letter Nineteen

This piece was omitted from 2e.
°3e.
1. In 4e, Shklovsky has made the question of authorship less ambiguous by adding: "It's Alya's letter."

Letter Nineteen

This letter was omitted from 2e.
1. The Wertheim, a large department store in Berlin.

Letter Twenty

This letter was omitted from 2e, 3e, 4e.

Letter Twenty-one

This letter was omitted from 2e.

Letter Twenty-two

1. A *lazzo* is a comic routine or dialogue that was used in the commedia dell'arte to interrupt the proceedings at strategic moments.

Letter Twenty-three

This letter was omitted from 2e.
°3e, 4e.

1. First line of a famous lyrical digression from Gogol's short story "Strashnaia mest'" [A Terrible Vengeance], from volume II of the cycle known as *Vechera na khutore bliz Dikan'ki* [Evenings on a Farm near Dikanka] (St. Petersburg, 1832).

Letter Twenty-four

1. Marc Chagall (b. 1889). Chagall left Vitebsk in 1907 to study at the art academy in Petersburg. Between 1911 and 1914, he studied in Paris, returning to Russia after the outbreak of World War I. After the revolution, he was appointed director of the new art school in Vitebsk, a position which he held until difficulties developed with the painter Malevich, whom he had invited to the school. He then went to Moscow and became scenic designer for the State Jewish Theater. When disagreements developed with the regime, he emigrated, spending a few months in Berlin in 1922 before settling in Paris.
°4e.

2. When the White army commanded by General Wrangel was trapped in the Crimea by the advancing Red Army in October 1920, British ships rescued the men and carried them to Constantinople.

3. Nikolai Nikolaevich Evreinov (1879–1953), noted playwright, as well as theoretician and historian of the drama. He was expelled from Russia in the fall of 1922.

4. The terms of this paragraph, though outwardly similar, are predicated on radically different facts. Kiev, Feodosia, and Tiflis mushroomed not because the Bolsheviks converted them into cultural centers, but because they were centers of resistance to the Bolshevik regime and havens for large numbers of fugitives.

°4e.

5. Folk motifs, such as those found in gaily decorated barbershop signs, were an important inspiration for avant-garde Russian painters during the second decade of the twentieth century.

6. Russian cabarets in Berlin.

7. Shibboleth of the Serapion Brothers. It supplied the title for a recent book of memoirs by the former Serapion Veniamin Kaverin: *Zdravstvui, brat. Pisat' ochen' trudno* [Hi, Brother. Writing's Far from Easy] (Moscow, 1965).

Letter Twenty-five

1. Ilya Grigorievich Ehrenburg (1891–1967), prolific novelist and journalist. During the civil-war period, Ehrenburg sympathized with the Whites and seriously contemplated emigration, but after the defeat of Wrangel's White army in the fall of 1920, he returned to Moscow. In the spring of 1921, he was sent abroad as a foreign correspondent for Soviet publications. Expelled from France after being denounced to the police as a dangerous Bolshevik (by Aleksei Tolstoy, according to Nina Berberova), he spent the summer in Belgium, where he wrote *Julio Jurenito*, then moved to Berlin, where he remained until 1923.

°2e.

2. Ehrenburg and the painter El Lissitzky (1890–1941) published three issues of *Veshch'* [Object] during 1922 in Russian, French, and German. It was the first international publication of the seminal constructivist movement. As an organ of the movement's radical faction, it stressed the irrelevance of pure art to the modern world and advocated the cultivation of utilitarian art forms—industrial design, architecture, films, posters.

3. *Neobyknovennye prikliucheniia Khulio Khurenito i ego uchenikov* [The Unusual Adventures of Julio Jurenito and His Disciples] (Berlin, 1922), which most critics consider Ehrenburg's best book.

4. *Trest D. E.: Istoriia gibeli Evropy* [Trust D. E.: A History of the Demise of Europe] (Berlin, 1923).

5. Cunégonde's fond memory of the Bulgarian captain actually occurs during her first reunion with Candide—in chapter eight, where she is still young and beautiful, though slightly frayed.

6. From the Decameron: seventh story of the second day.

Letter Twenty-six

1. Propadaite te dorozhki
   Po kotorym ia khodil!

Shklovsky seems to be paraphrasing a well-known *chastushka:*

   Pozarostali stezhki-dorozhki,
   Gde prokhodili milogo nozhki,
   Pozarostali mokhom travoiu,
   Gde my guliali, milyi s toboiu.

[The paths where my dearest and I used to stroll are now overgrown with moss and grass.]

2. This is an untranslatable pun in Russian. The Russian word for "gigolo" is "al'fons," which circulated throughout the nineteenth century, but became current after 1874, when the comedy *Monsieur Alphonse*, by Dumas *fils*, was produced in Russia. As used in the letter, the word acquires a secondary referent—Alfonso XIII, King of Spain between 1886 and 1931. The Hispano-Suiza was a Spanish automobile manufactured

for the very rich; the first models, made in 1904, were
sold to King Alfonso XIII, and the company named its 1912
model after him.

3. In 1909, one model won the Coupe de l'Auto Race in
France.

Letter Twenty-seven

1. In 4e, the following passage has been added:

Don't be angry with the mouse, Alya.
The heart is studded with copper buttons, like the jacket of an
elevator boy.
Each day, it lifts a thousand times and falls a thousand times.
It's like a mouse embossed by the mousetrap.
I love you—as the sun is loved. As the wind is loved. As the
mountains are loved.
As they are loved: for all time.

Letter Twenty-eight

This letter was omitted from 2e.
°3e, 4e.

Letter Twenty-nine

°4e.

1. Russian troops, under the command of General Yudenich,
captured the supposedly impregnable fortress of Erzerum on
February 16, 1916, after a five-day siege, in the course of
which more than 10,000 Turks were killed. Shklovsky's friend

is Ilya Mikhailovich Zdanevich (b. 1894), a futurist poet, dramatist, and theoretician, now living in Paris.

°4e.

Preface to the Second Edition

This preface was omitted from 4e.

Preface to the Third Edition

In 4e, Shklovsky entitled this preface "Second Preface to an Old Book," and he added at the bottom: "Leningrad, 1924," although it is actually the third preface and was written for the 1929 edition.

°4e.

1. In 4e, the following words were added: "I was poor. I bought roses—instead of bread."

°I was . . . . 4e.

°Now I . . . . 4e.

2. In 4e, the first "old friend" is replaced by "guilty one"; the words "and sentimental. Live on, old friend" are omitted; and the phrase "I will not revise you" has been changed to: "I cannot re-educate you."

3. In 4e, the following sentence has been added: "Sleep doesn't erase the memory of my tresses, even though they've turned white." In 5e, this postscript is omitted entirely (the only point at which 4e and 5e differ).

Second Preface to the Fourth Edition

1. A reference to *Letters from My Mill* (1869), the unorthodox epistolary work by Alphonse Daudet.

2. These lines draw upon the numerous Russian folk tales about miracle-working fish (i.e., "At the Pike's Command" and Pushkin's "Tale of the Fisherman and the Fish"), as well as the folk tales about magic rings lost in the depths of the sea (i.e., "Martin the Peasant's Son").

3. This sentence, echoing a couplet frequently cited by Shklovsky in his later books, comes from the poem "The Paradox of Time," by Henry Austin Dobson (1840–1921):

> Time goes, you say? Ah no!
> Alas, Time stays, *we* go.

Letter Thirty

This letter, entitled "Introductory Letter," appeared in 2e and 3e; it was drastically abbreviated in 4e.

1. Corporal punishment was abolished in the Soviet Union soon after the revolution.

2. Part II, chap. xx.

3. The success of the February revolution depended on gaining the support of the Petrograd garrison. After the first few days of unrest, the Pavlovsky Regiment joined the insurgents on February 28; the Volhynian and Lithuanian Regiments followed suit on the next day.

4. The abortive Decembrist revolt took place in December 1825.

°4e.

5. Baku, an important oil center, was captured by the Turks in September 1918.

Letter Thirty-one

This letter appeared only in 2e (Letter 14) and 3e (26).

1. *Istoriia russkoi intelligentsii deviatnadtsatogo veka*, a work

published in 1911 by the distinguished critic Dmitry Nikolaevich Ovsyaniko-Kulikovsky (1853–1920). Quite uninterested in questions of style and structure, Ovsyaniko-Kulikovsky stressed the psychological and sociological components of literature. He viewed art as a product of spiritual activity which gives an individual interpretation of eternal values and problems; he studied characters and authors from the standpoint of how they embody the salient traits of their epochs—all of which made him quite foreign to Shklovsky.

2. In 3e, the following sentence was added: "That's why it was left out of the first edition."

3. Tatyana appears in Pushkin's *Evgenii Onegin;* Vera in Lermontov's *A Hero of Our Time;* Bolkonsky in Tolstoy's *War and Peace.*

Letter Thirty-two

This letter appeared in 2e (Letter 17), 3e (18), and 4e (18).

Letter Thirty-three

This letter appeared in 2e (Letter 17), 3e (18), and 4e (18).

1. One small, but essential, change has been made in 4e: the period at the end of "I love you" has been converted into a comma, and the signature "Alya" has been placed after the comma; hence, the sentiment attributed to Alya in 2e and 3e is assumed by Shklovsky in 4e.

Letter Thirty-four

This letter appeared in 2e (Letter 21), 3e (30), and 4e (28). It first appeared, in substantially the same form, under the

title "Chuzhaia skazka" [A Foreign Fairy Tale] in *Zhizn'*
iskusstva [The Life of Art], I (January 1, 1924), p. 8.

1. In 3e, the following sentence was added: "The letter wasn't
written down at the time, but words unuttered have a way of
becoming thoughts."

2. A reference to an anecdote quoted by Shklovsky in his
book *The Third Factory*, pp. 39–40. The anecdote is from
chapter xii of Tolstoy's work *Chto zhe nam delat'* [What Must
We Do?].

I remember walking down the street once in Moscow and seeing
a man step outside ahead of me and peer at the stones in the
sidewalk; then he selected one stone, crouched over it and began
(or so it seemed to me) to scrape or rub with singular strain and
effort.
"What is he doing to that sidewalk?," I thought. When I got
right up to him, I saw what this man was doing. It was a young
man from the butcher shop: he was sharpening his knife against a
stone in the sidewalk. He was not thinking about the stones at all,
though he was scrutinizing them; still less was he thinking about
them while performing his task—he was sharpening his knife. He
had to sharpen his knife in order to cut meat; it had seemed to me
that he was performing this task over the stones in the sidewalk.
In exactly the same way, man seems to be occupied with
commerce, treaties, wars, the arts and the sciences when one thing
matters to him and one thing is all he does: he tries to clarify
the moral laws by which he lives.

3. This is a rather free adaptation of the fairy tale entitled
"The Swineherd," by Hans Christian Andersen.

Postscript

This piece, written after Shklovsky returned to Russia, was
inserted in the second edition of *A Sentimental Journey*
(Leningrad, 1924), pp. 185–186.

1. *Za chertopolokhom,* published in Berlin during 1922 and written by Pyotr Nikolaevich Krasnov (1869–1947), former White general and ataman of the Don Cossacks.

2. There were several communist-inspired rebellions against the German government between 1919 and 1923, the most notable being the Spartacus uprising in January 1919, the brief establishment of a communist republic in Bavaria in April 1919, and the Hamburg uprising in October 1923. All these rebellions were ruthlessly suppressed by the government.

3. In January 1923, France, declaring that Germany had defaulted in her reparations obligations, occupied the Ruhr and proceeded to have the coal from these mines diverted to France—an act which brought Germany to the brink of economic collapse and civil war.

Index of Names

SELECTED DALKEY ARCHIVE PAPERBACKS

FOR A FULL LIST OF PUBLICATIONS, VISIT:
www.dalkeyarchive.com

SELECTED  PAPERBACKS

FOR A FULL LIST OF PUBLICATIONS, VISIT:
www.dalkeyarchive.com